"How many cases don't get resolved?" retired Detective Isadora Fawn asked an instant before her new partner, retired Detective Hugh Halligan, could.

"We have five unresolved cases on the bar in the meeting room," the Task Force leader, Andor, said. "We keep them there to remind us to not forget the people involved in them."

"Only five since the start of the task force?" Halligan asked.

"Since the start," Andor said, nodding.

"No pressure," Fawn said.

Andor reached into a case beside his chair and pulled out a folder that looked like an official case file with "Copy" stamped in big letters on it. He slid it toward Halligan. "My money is on this being the sixth. Just not much there. No offense to you two."

Halligan glanced at the name on the file.

Sandy Goodson.

Damn it all to hell.

Halligan knew Andor was right because Halligan had been on that case in his early days as a detective. Halligan's name would be the lead detective in that file for that poor woman who had just vanished into thin air.

Halligan glanced at Fawn who clearly also knew the old case. Neither of them had touched the file on the table.

Then Halligan looked back at Andor. "Don't suppose we can get a mulligan on this one?"

Andor laughed.

But Halligan had been quite serious.

ALSO BY DEAN WESLEY SMITH

BOTTOM PAIR

A Cold Poker Gang Mystery

DEAN WESLEY SMITH

Bottom Pair

First published in a different form in *Smith's Monthly* #49, May 2021
Published by WMG Publishing
Cover and Layout copyright © 2021 by WMG Publishing
Cover design by Allyson Longueira/WMG Publishing
Cover art copyright © Arsgera/Depositphotos
ISBN-13: 978-1-56146-485-2
ISBN-10: 1-56146-485-6

BOTTOM PAIR

Bottom Pair:

When a player in a hand has a pair, but the pair is smaller than another player's pair, the losing hand is called a bottom pair.

PROLOGUE

March 18th, 2002
Henderson, Nevada

Sandy Goodson loved the early mornings in Henderson. Especially in the spring when it hadn't gotten too hot yet. From the front door of her three-bedroom home in the Deep Canyon Heights subdivision, she could see the casinos of the Strip in Las Vegas stretching away from her.

The sun, just peaking over the hills to the east, lit the casinos up like beacons in the early morning light.

She loved the home that she had just bought last year, even though at the moment it felt too big for her. She loved the Strip, and she loved working there. She couldn't believe how lucky she had gotten to get a job in hospitality at the Luxor Hotel. A dream job that paid her a lot for doing what she loved, helping people and talking with them. And it gave her a chance to meet people; people who have ended up important in her life.

She stood on her front porch enjoying the coolness of the

1

morning air for a minute, going through her normal checklist, making sure she was ready. She stood five-five, had long blonde hair that while working she kept pulled back and away from her face.

Susan, her best friend in the entire world, said she looked wonderful with her hair pulled back or down around her face. Sandy trusted Susan and just thinking of her made Sandy smile.

Sandy checked her purple uniform, a color that didn't go well with her pale skin, but other employees she worked with said just wait and that will change. The Luxor always switched out their uniforms every six months or so. She didn't worry about it at this point.

She had on sneakers that she would change out for high heels as soon as she got to the employee locker room, and she checked to make sure her dress shoes were in her bag. They were.

And her Luxor ID was in her bag along with her purse.

Everything exactly as she always did every morning. Nothing at all different. She had made sure of that.

She was ready, keys in her hand, so she pulled closed and locked her front door, not letting herself look back.

With one last look at the Strip in the distance, she climbed into her white 2001 Subaru that she called Horse that she had bought for herself when she got the job at the Luxor.

She pulled out of her driveway, the streets of the subdivision deserted in the early morning hours. She went past the security cameras at the front gate at almost exactly the same time she did every morning and turned right toward the Strip.

She was smiling, anticipating and yet worried about the day ahead of her.

That was the last anyone ever saw of her.

She vanished without a trace, and six months later her

missing person's case went cold and she was pretty much forgotten.

Two years later her younger sister, Reese, sold Sandy's car, which was found parked on a side street just off the Strip. Because of the mortgage payments, Reese also sold Sandy's wonderful house.

But Reese never stopped looking for Sandy. It seemed that for almost twenty years, Reese was the only one.

CHAPTER ONE

February 21st, 2019
Las Vegas, Nevada

Retired Detective Isadora Fawn leaned against her blue Jeep SUV in the older downtown Las Vegas neighborhood. No one ever called her Isadora. She only answered to Fawn.

Fawn to her friends. Detective Fawn to everyone else.

The sun had just gone down behind the mountains to the west and the air had a crisp bite to it, something she actually liked. She had on a light-blue windbreaker over a brand new white silk blouse, a new pair of her standard jeans, and new running shoes. This was her version of dressing up. And the jacket kept her more than warm enough in the cool evening air.

She enjoyed this time of the year far more than she liked the intense summer heat. Luckily, the temperatures in Vegas were only really hot for three months, so the other nine months were heaven.

As she looked down the darkening neighborhood street lined

by large old oak and maple trees, a car came toward her. She could tell it was a Cadillac SUV, black and brand new. It still had the dealer plate on it. That was recently retired Detective Hugh Halligan's new car, bought two weeks ago for himself when he retired.

She had laughed when he had called her and told her what he had done and insisted on taking her for a ride to lunch to celebrate. She had to be honest, she loved the car as well and she had a hunch she would be riding in it a lot. And helping Halligan figure out all the new devices it offered.

They had been friends for decades, but never really worked together. A decade or so ago, she and her ex-husband and he and his late wife had done a lot of concerts and dinners together. They were great fun until Halligan's wife Cindy started into her losing battle with breast cancer and Fawn's husband found a blackjack dealer at the MGM Grand more interesting than his wife.

Luckily, Fawn had gotten out of that mess before his gambling broke them, and before her father died and left her more money than she actually knew what to do with. Not a dime of it had gone to "the cheating bastard" as she called her ex.

She had no intent of ever saying his real name again.

Or seeing him again for that matter.

You just didn't cheat on a well-known Las Vegas police detective and think you could get away with it. This town might appear big to tourists, but in reality it just wasn't that big. Not cheating big.

It had been two years since the divorce was final and she had enjoyed every moment of those two years away from him. She hadn't realized just how much she had grown to dislike the guy while they were married.

She had done nothing with her money from first the divorce and then from her father's estate, other than be surprised at how much it was. She liked her old Jeep and her condo in a small complex in Henderson. Both paid off. The money from her father and no bills allowed her the freedom to retire at age 55 and join the Cold Poker Gang task force.

Plus she got a pension from the city for her thirty years on the force which, actually, was more than enough to live on as well.

Halligan was actually age 55 as well and had always had family money as long as she had known him, plus he told her that Cindy had a massive life insurance policy when she died three years ago. Now he also had his pension for his thirty-one years.

Halligan and Cindy had lived in a big five-bedroom mini-mansion in an exclusive subdivision in Henderson and Halligan had just never moved out after Cindy's death. Fawn would have to ask him what he did with all that room at some point.

She watched as Halligan carefully parked his new car in front of hers and behind a car she knew belonged to retired Detective Cavanaugh. From the looks of the other cars on the street, some that she recognized, a bunch of the Cold Poker Gang task force were already here ahead of them.

Halligan got out, locked up the car and strode toward her, smiling.

He was a stocky man, more square than anything, but not fat in any way. Still very handsome, even though he was going bald. In the summer the top of his head tended to glow red, something she had often teased him about. He always said he was attempting to imitate her red hair. Standing joke.

They were both in great shape since both spent time in the

gym every week and he did a lot of walking while she ran for exercise most mornings.

She always felt so at ease with Halligan, which is why they had decided to retire at the same time after talking with Andor, the retired detective who ran the Cold Poker Gang task force, about teaming up for the task force.

Andor had loved the idea, so now, two weeks after they both had retired, they were about to go to their first task force meeting, get their first case.

"You excited?" Hugh asked, stopping in front of her. A smile as big as she had seen on his face since before Cindy got sick.

Fawn laughed. "Excited to be able to work on cases at my own speed, on my own time, and not have to do paperwork. Of course I'm excited."

He pretended to frown, but Fawn knew it was fake.

"You mean you're not excited to partner with me?"

She laughed again and took his arm and turned him toward the house with all the lights on and cars in the driveway. "Come on you big lug, let's go see what we're got ourselves into."

"Hot damn," he said.

And laughing, they headed across the street and to their first Cold Poker Gang task force meeting.

CHAPTER TWO

February 21st, 2019
Las Vegas, Nevada

Retired Detective Hugh Halligan let his friend and soon to be partner, Fawn, lead him up the stairs, through the front door, and into the front room of the house. The living room was comfortable, in browns and tan tones, comfortable cloth furniture, and a big screen television on one wall. Two full bookcases filled areas between the living room and the dining room, making the two rooms clearly separate, yet open to each other.

It was a remodeled design from a 1930s home. Halligan liked it. Felt homey. Far more so than his big, mostly empty small mansion out in Henderson.

Retired detectives Bayard Lott and Julia Rogers owned the place and hosted the weekly meetings in their game room downstairs. It used to be Lott's and his previous wife's place and then a few years after his wife died, he and Julia had become an item and married a year or so ago, with half of Las Vegas's finest coming to the wedding. Clearly Julia and Lott spent their share of time in this very comfortable living room.

But what surprised Halligan more than anything was the intense smell of KFC. Wow, he had had a small snack before coming and now he was instantly hungry.

"I was warned about that smell," Fawn said, shaking her head. "Guess it is the ritual of Lott and Julia and Andor to meet over KFC before every Cold Poker Gang meeting."

"Damn," Halligan said, "I'm going to need dinner when this is over."

"You and me both," Fawn said.

They followed the sounds of talking and laughing to a staircase leading to the basement just off the dining room. At first glance as they went down the wide stairs, Halligan could tell there were a good twenty detectives in the room, most sitting around two poker tables, very intent on the game and their cards.

"Looks like the task force is named correctly," Fawn said.

Halligan could only agree to that.

The room clearly had been remodeled and expanded and actually didn't even seem that crowded even with two standard poker tables in it. Impressive private game room, maybe the best he had ever seen, and that was going some in Las Vegas.

Standing off to one side of the room near a bar were retired detectives Benson Cavanaugh and Bonnie State, talking with Andor. Up until tonight, they were the two newest detectives to join the task force. Now that distinction went to Fawn and Halligan. As one friend had called them, "the bottom pair."

Andor looked up and saw them and smiled. He was a solid guy, about five-five, with a bald head and a loose-fitting gray sports coat. But he radiated power and command. And when he walked, it was more like a bull going through whatever was in his way.

"Hey, everyone," Andor said into all the noise, his voice carrying power that stopped all the talking almost instantly, "welcome our two new recruits. And our newest team. Detectives Fawn and Halligan."

Everyone applauded and a few cheered as both of them took a bow. Halligan was impressed he and Fawn managed to do it at the same time and in the same way.

Halligan knew half of the detectives in the room and got a hunch he would know the other half by names and reputation once he met them.

For the next hour, he and Fawn talked with a lot of people. Enjoying every minute of it since this wasn't about work or some case, but just all retired detectives enjoying a night out.

They called this a "meeting" but there clearly was no structured "meeting" about it. Basically the task force met to play poker and just be with each other.

He and Fawn ended up with Cavanaugh and State and Andor standing near the bar. The poker games were about to go down to one table as detectives staggered out, not drunk, just beyond some of their bed times.

Cavanaugh was a thin, in-shape kind of guy who towered over most people. He had piercing green eyes, a bald head, and usually wore a sloppy sports jacket a few sizes too big to make him look shambling. Tonight he had on a new tan jacket that fit him and made him look dapper instead of shambling.

Detective Bonnie State had short brown hair, deep brown eyes, a long face and she had to be almost six feet tall as well. Standing beside Cavanaugh, she was slightly shorter, but together they were an imposing team. Halligan, Fawn, and Andor looked tiny standing with them.

"Normally I give out the first case here at the meeting," Andor said. "But need to get you two new recruits some help first. So would you mind if the five of us met tomorrow for lunch at the Main Street Station buffet? Say 1 p.m.?"

Cavanaugh and State just shrugged, looked at each other, and nodded at the same time. Halligan was surprised that two of the most independent detectives on the force were now clearly a couple. They had only been retired a few months.

"Fine by me," Fawn said.

Halligan shrugged and said, "Sure."

He had no idea what kind of help he and Fawn might need, but it would be a fun lunch no matter what.

About twenty minutes later, he and Fawn headed back up the stairs. The intense smell of KFC was now only in the background, but enough to remind Halligan that he was hungry.

"You up for some pizza on the way home?" he asked as he and Fawn went out into the brisk night air.

"Would love some," Fawn said, smiling. "Sounds perfect."

"Late enough that most of the tourists will be beyond dinner," Halligan said.

"Slice of New York" at Mandalay Bay?" Fawn asked, smiling at him.

"Damn, now you're reading my mind," he said, laughing. "Meet you on the third floor of the Mandalay Bay parking garage."

"Right or left side?"

"Left as you go up the escalator," he said.

"Perfect," she said as she headed for her car.

And the pizza was perfect, as was the company.

By the time (two hours later) that he finally got home, he knew for sure that he had made the right decision to retire. And working with Fawn was just going to be a lot of fun.

And after the last ten years and then losing Cindy, he deserved some fun in his life.

CHAPTER THREE

February 22nd, 2019
Las Vegas, Nevada

Fawn was still floating from the evening before when Halligan pulled up in front of her building to pick her up for lunch. They had decided over pizza last night that he loved to drive and she could take it or leave it, so he would be their primary driver in his new Cadillac SUV.

"Unless you suck at it," Fawn had said. "No chance I want to ride around scared out of my wits every day."

"Deal," Halligan said, laughing. "If I suck, you drive."

Fawn had a hunch he was a damn fine driver. Halligan pretty much did everything to the best of his ability. Something she had admired about him for decades now.

Around her the air was cool, but the sky was typical Las Vegas deep blue. A slight breeze disturbed the trees, but nothing bad at all. Just another perfect Las Vegas winter day.

She had on her normal jeans, cotton blouse, tennis shoes,

and had a light windbreaker over the top that hid her badge on her belt and her gun in a holster under her arm. No one took her for a detective because of her shortness and red hair and she had used that element of surprise more than she could count.

This morning Halligan had on jeans, tennis shoes, what looked to be a dress shirt, and a Vegas Knights jacket that also clearly hid his badge and gun. She would bet anything that he wasn't a hockey fan, but had just got the jacket cheap.

She climbed into the passenger seat and he waited for her to get the seat into position and her belt on before he swung the car around and headed back toward the freeway to take them downtown.

In five minutes he had effortlessly got them into freeway traffic and moving along at seventy, which felt in this new Cadillac like it wasn't moving much at all. Amazingly comfortable. In her older Jeep, seventy felt like it was a little bit of a strain. Maybe it was time to trade in for a newer car.

Maybe.

She'd have to think about it more.

But so far he was clearly an experienced and comfortable driver and she liked that.

She had no idea when they actually left the city of Henderson and went into Las Vegas. Henderson had become the second largest city in the state, but was just basically part of Las Vegas, sitting on the southwest side, filling most of the area between Interstate 15 and Boulder City. Of course it had never mattered to her since it was all in Clark County and the police departments of all the towns in Clark County decades before had become the Las Vegas Metro.

"So what is this help Andor thinks we need to get started?" Halligan asked. "Any ideas?"

"Wondered about that all morning," Fawn said. Even

though she hadn't gotten to bed until after midnight, she had still made her seven am morning run and yoga exercises when she got home. During that entire time she tried to figure out that exact question.

She had worked alone for the last years as an active detective and so had Halligan. And they both had seemed to do just fine without any more help than the department gave them.

After her run and breakfast, she had cleared out old files from her desk and got ready, she hoped, to handle new cases. Because she had worked solo, she hadn't spent much time at her desk in the station, so she wasn't going to miss that. Instead she had mostly worked out of her office in a second bedroom in her condo.

It had felt good to clear that out this morning. Felt like she was starting over, starting something new, and that had her more excited than she wanted to admit.

"The task force certainly seems to pull off a lot of almost miraculous case solutions at times," Halligan said. "Solutions active detectives never got to. Maybe this morning they are going to give us the secret magic potion."

"I was figuring it had to be drugs to make people tell the truth to old cops," Fawn said.

"Yeah, that's it," Halligan said, pretending to be serious. "We put it in bottles of water and offer it to them."

"Or you hold them down and I force it into them," Fawn said.

"Nope, you get to hold them down," Halligan said. "Last time I had to hold a perp down, I sprained a knee and walked funny for a week."

"You still walk funny," she said, laughing.

He pretended to be hurt.

Damn, working with Halligan was going to be fun. She was

already feeling better about retiring. She had had to make a change after the last two years recovering from "the cheating bastard." And an old friend like Halligan was just the medicine for that.

In less than 15 minutes, which had to be a record from Henderson to downtown Las Vegas, Halligan pulled into the Main Street Station Casino and Hotel parking lot and shut off the engine.

"Well," she said, as they both climbed out of the car into the cool afternoon air. "You don't suck."

He laughed and bowed slightly. "I will take any compliment I can get from you."

"Don't expect them too often," she said.

"Oh, I wouldn't think of it," he said.

They both laughed as they crossed Main Street to the casino, arm in arm.

CHAPTER FOUR

February 22nd, 2019
Las Vegas, Nevada

Halligan hadn't been in the old Main Street Station Casino much over the years. He lived out in Henderson, was stationed out that way, and unless there was a reason on a case, never got downtown much at all. And years ago, the downtown area had been more like a war zone, with empty buildings, more homeless than tourists, and no reason to be there. But in the last ten years it had really been revamped and showed nothing but promise going forward.

The downtown area now actually had a good feel to it and they had just knocked down an entire city block along Fremont where some of the worst places had been, including The Gentleman's Club Hotel and Casino, which toward the end of its life was far from that description.

Inside the casino, the Main Street Station had been decorated to look like an old train station from the 1930s. Amazing antiques filled different areas, including a row of antique slot machines on display. The high ceilings were held up with thick, polished wooden beams and all the windows were ornate glass, many of them stained glass. The Main Street Station was one of the few hotels and casinos he had seen with actual windows.

"Wow," Fawn said, looking around. "This place is really old school."

"Never been in here before?" Halligan asked, surprised.

"First time," Fawn said, just sort of staring around at the amazing décor.

"Wait until you see the buffet."

It took them a moment to get through a few crowds of tourists and bunches of slot machines before finding the massive buffet tucked off to the north side of the large main casino floor behind a large wall of windows and a very long bar.

Like the casino and main lobby area, the buffet had thirty- or forty-foot high ceilings, all wood beamed, and plants filled different areas and hung from the rafters. Expensive antique furniture sat in places, including a massive old oak antique table right in the middle of the entrance.

On one side of one of the huge rooms, the buffet itself seemed to stretch for a half mile, disappearing around a corner in the room.

From what Halligan could tell, there had to be a good hundred tables in the main room, a secondary area he could see beyond a massive desert bar area, and a third room on the other side where the buffet went around the corner and into the distance there.

"A complete classic old-style Vegas buffet," Halligan said to Fawn as they paid. Just $11 each for lunch. That was insanely cheap.

Halligan could see that Andor, Cavanaugh, and State were

already sitting at a large table in a corner on the far side of the room, along with a younger man. They were already all eating.

"We late?" Fawn asked as she led Halligan through the tables toward the group.

"Actually we're five minutes early," Halligan said. "I'm starting to think that all the members of this task force are over-achievers."

Fawn laughed. "Or just really hungry."

"Could be that," Halligan agreed.

The group waved and Andor pointed toward the buffet, so Halligan and Fawn detoured to get food.

Ten minutes later they were both back at the table with far too much food on both of their plates. Halligan had walked the entire buffet first, then gone back for things he really wanted to try. Fawn had just seen something she wanted and went from there. Halligan had a hunch that was going to be their working styles as well.

"This place is amazing," Fawn said as they got settled.

"Since we all live close," State said, "this is a favorite meeting spot."

"Worth driving in from Henderson for," Halligan said.

Fawn nodded to that as she started eating.

Andor introduced the young man at the table as Jacob State, Bonnie's son. To Halligan, Jacob looked hidden, and from the backpack he had on the floor beside his chair and the hoodie he was wearing, someone like Jacob could just vanish into any crowd if he wanted.

After they had all eaten for a few minutes, Andor said, "Welcome aboard, you two. Can't begin to tell you how happy we are to have you join the task force. We've lost five of the original gang just the last three months, so you four are a godsend."

Halligan took his water glass and raised it into the air for Fawn and Cavanaugh and State. "To being a godsend."

All four of them laughed and toasted that.

"So what's this help you think we need?" Fawn asked.

Jacob, without missing a bite from the disappearing mound of food on his plate, raised his hand.

Halligan had no clue what that meant and clearly neither did Fawn.

"Let me explain," Andor said. "Back when I first convinced the Chief that Lott and Rogers and I should form this task force, it became very, very clear quickly that good old-fashioned foot-work was good, but not good enough in this modern world to solve cold cases."

Halligan nodded to that.

"So Lott and Julia, through Lott's daughter Annie, knew a guy by the name of Mike," Andor said. "Mike was a flat magi-cian with computers and still is. And he also has a bodyguard service for the rich and famous that consists of ex-special services."

"Are they the ones that cleared the tunnels of that sex ring," Fawn said, "before even SWAT went in."

Andor nodded. "Exactly. It was the task force team of Pickett and Sarge and Robin who broke that. They have Robin's husband and his private security company to help them as well. Robin is also a magician with computers and she has people at her husband's company that are amazing as well."

"I can vouch for that," Jacob said. "I freelance for them at times when they need help."

"And Jacob here is helping his mother and Cavanaugh," Andor said. "He has clearance to get into any police file in the nation, pretty much, and has a network of top people he can work with around the country."

"You cannot believe how good footwork combined with great computer skills can open up things that didn't seem possible to open just a few years before," Cavanaugh said.

Beside him, State nodded.

"So this is why the Cold Poker Gang Task Force has been so successful in closing cases?" Fawn asked. "We were guessing it was because you fed people truth drugs."

Everyone laughed.

"This is a ton better," Andor said. "And why the Chief loves us, lets us carry badges and our guns, and not do paperwork."

"Clearly I need to be paid more," Jacob said, focusing on clearing off the last bit from his plate.

"You don't get paid anything," State said, laughing and patting her son's arm. "None of us do."

"Oh, yeah," Jacob said, smiling at his mother.

"So Jacob has volunteered to help you two when you need it," Andor said.

Jacob nodded. "I've followed you both for some time. Impressed at how you handle cases and people. And Detective Fawn, Mom and Cavanaugh here told me how professionally you handled that case out of the old hotel, and yet kept them involved. And the serial killer one with the cancer doc. So when she told me you two were joining the task force, I offered to help."

"Thank you," Fawn said. "And you were the Jacob that saved us out there at the cat place?"

"I guess so," Jacob said.

"He did," Bonnie said, smiling at her son.

Halligan could tell that Jacob was slightly embarrassed.

"Are you sure you have the time?" Halligan asked.

Jacob laughed. "I've helped them on two cases so far. In four weeks it has taken me all of five hours max. I spend more time working for the Chief and freelancing with Mike's people and Robin's husband's company than anything else. Plus I now have help. Judy Young, who is Officer Young's granddaughter. She's going to be as good as I am pretty soon. We work together a lot."

Halligan nodded. He and Young had become friends over the years, but Halligan hadn't seen him much since their wives both got sick and then died. "How is Young these days?"

"Working on him to join this task force," Andor said.

Jacob nodded. "Judy and I make a point to get him out of the house every week. He's coming around."

"We'll stop and give him a hard time," Fawn said. "Maybe we can get him to help us on whatever case you're going to give us."

Andor laughed, not a sound Halligan was sure he liked in this context.

"The rule," Andor said, "is that cases get put out in the order they come up from the Chief. He picks them, hands them to me, I give them out to the team who is next up, who has either given up on a case or has solved their previous assignment."

"How many cases don't get resolved?" Fawn asked an instant before Halligan could.

"We have five unresolved cases on the bar in the meeting room," Andor said. "We keep them there to remind us to not forget the people involved in them.

"Only five since the start of the task force?" Halligan asked.

"Since the start," Andor said, nodding.

"No pressure," Fawn said.

Andor reached into a case beside his chair and pulled out a folder that looked like an official case file with "Copy" stamped in big letters on it. He slid it toward Halligan. "My money is on this being the sixth. Just not much there. No offense to you two."

Halligan glanced at the name on the file.

Sandy Goodson.

Damn it all to hell.

Halligan knew Andor was right, there wasn't much there because Halligan had been on that case in his early days as a detective. Halligan's name would be the lead detective in that file for that poor woman who just vanished into thin air.

Halligan glanced at Fawn who clearly also knew the old case. Neither of them had touched the file on the table.

Then Halligan looked back at Andor. "Don't suppose we can get a mulligan on this one?"

Andor, Cavanaugh, and State laughed.

Halligan had been serious.

CHAPTER FIVE

February 22nd, 2019
Las Vegas, Nevada

Fawn sat with the thin file on her lap as Halligan pulled out of the Main Street Station Casino and headed for the freeway. Both of them were silent. Fawn didn't even need to open the file. She had been assigned to take a look at this case about fifteen years ago.

Nothing came of it.

Sandy Goodson had just flat vanished without a trace on her way to work early one morning. Her car was found a few days later after Sandy's sister filed a missing person's report.

Halligan had been the lead detective at the time of the disappearance and it was Sandy's sister Reese that got Fawn assigned to take a look five years later.

Besides a short report saying that she had found nothing, Fawn knew she hadn't added a detail to the case at all. There was a reason the file on her lap was so thin. The facts were even thinner.

"So got any ideas of what we are going to do?" Halligan said.

Fawn shook her head. "Not a damn thought at all."

"Well, we got expert computer help now," Halligan said. "Is Jacob really that good?"

"From what Cavanaugh and State said on those last two cases, he is," she said. "When we were in the basement of that old hotel he pulled up the original construction plans of the place within minutes which helped us find a hidden room. Then on that last case he managed to warn all three of us out of a building, more than likely saved our lives."

"So you trust him?" Halligan said.

"I do," Fawn said. "And clearly the chief does as well. Plus he has high level security clearance just about everywhere."

"So that's something we didn't have when we looked at this case the first times."

"You know I went over it?" Fawn asked, surprised.

Halligan nodded. "That damn case has woken me up in a cold sweat more times than not over the last twenty years. It was one of my first, didn't get solved, so I dug out the file every few years just to see."

"So it's our first on the task force," Fawn said. "Let's go for a different result."

"Agreed," Halligan said.

They sat quietly for the next ten minutes as Halligan got them out past the Strip and on Interstate 215 going into Henderson. Fawn had no idea where they were headed. Seemed like they were both a little in shock and Halligan had them just headed home.

"You know Skimos Coffee Shop on Sunset?" Fawn asked. It

was considered the best little coffee shop in all of Las Vegas and Fawn had never had a reason to argue with that reputation.

"I do," he said. "The one with the great Danish rolls? The manager keeps the back table in a side room reserved for me and whatever case file I am working on."

"Nope, he keeps that table for me," Fawn said, shaking her head. How the two of them hadn't worked together before this was a complete surprise.

"Well," said Halligan, "we got a case file and we need to work. "You up for sharing a table?"

"As long as I don't have to share my coffee," she said, laughing.

"No chance on that," Halligan said. "I order two so one is cool enough to drink fast by the time I get the first one done."

"Anyone ever tell you that you are nuts?"

"Yeah," Halligan said. "Pretty much every day."

CHAPTER SIX

February 22nd, 2019
Las Vegas, Nevada

Halligan really liked Skimos and it always seemed busy, which was why the manager let him come in, buy a snack and two coffees and sit in the back and work. Clearly he had done that for Fawn as well.

Ten minutes later Halligan found a place to park in the small lot and they were both standing in line at the art deco black and white main counter.

Besides the front counter, there was nothing really different about the place at all. All ten of the main tables in the small room were full and four of the tables outside along the edge of the parking lot also had people at them. Half the tables had laptops open on them. If the coffee and the pastries weren't so darned good, Halligan doubted he ever would have come here regularly.

But the coffee to die for and the private table in the small back room so he could work had made him a regular. Plus it wasn't that far from his house. He had no desire to add up how much he spent every month in Skimos. But it was no small amount.

Clearly Fawn had her habit here as well.

Ten minutes later they were at the table in the back, the manager happy to see them together.

They sat at the table so they could both look at the file together. Fawn had a legal pad and pen and he had a small notebook. He often made notes in the small notebook and then at home at night typed them up to see if he had missed something.

"So we're looking for some way to get an opening in this thing," Halligan said. "Maybe things that didn't exist twenty years ago."

"DNA," Fawn said. "I bet, if Sandy's sister is still alive, we can get a sample from her and have Jacob see if he can trace a family match."

Halligan nodded and wrote, feeling like at least they had something to add to the file.

Fawn took out her phone. "Going to call Jacob, ask him what is possible for him to do with DNA."

"Good idea," Halligan said.

As it started to ring, Fawn put the phone on speaker and put it between them. The noise from the talking in the main room was muffled enough that they would be able to hear just fine.

"Detective," Jacob said. "I was expecting your call once you dug into the case file."

"You have both of us here," Fawn said.

"From the sounds of it, you're at Skimos in that small back room," Jacob said.

"You tracking us?" Halligan asked.

"Nope," Jacob said. "That's just a favorite detective hangout in Henderson."

"Wow, are all detectives that predictable?" Fawn asked.

"Grew up with one, remember?" Jacob said. "And yes. So I bet you called about DNA."

"We did," Fawn said, looking up at Halligan and shaking her head.

Halligan was impressed, that was for sure.

"We were wondering what was possible for you to do," Fawn asked, "if we got a sample from our victim's sister?"

"I can look for a familial match pretty much worldwide," Jacob said. "I can get a sample, once you get it to me, processed in twenty-four hours. Won't hold on an evidence chain, but we can always repeat the process through a regular lab if we had to."

Halligan was fairly certain his mouth was hanging open. Normal police channels took weeks to months to get DNA processed, let alone do a worldwide search for matches.

"Wow," Halligan said. "Amazing."

"I agree," Fawn said. "Can you find us Reese Goodson's current address?"

"Hang on," Jacob said. Then a moment later he came back. "She's married to a Doctor Drakeson now. Lives in Henderson. Got two younger kids. I don't think she works at the moment, but has a master's in hospital administration."

He gave them the address and they both wrote it down.

"Thanks!" Halligan said.

"We'll contact you when we get the DNA," Fawn said.

"I also took the liberty of getting you all of Sandy Goodson's financial records from the time she disappeared and any activity on the accounts for a number of years afterward. Figured that might help some. Sent it to both your phones."

"You are amazing," Fawn said. "We hadn't gotten that far yet."

"Anything else Judy and I can do for you, just call."

With that he hung up.

Halligan just sat there shaking his head. It looked like the thickness of the Sandy Goodson file just doubled. And now he understood why Andor gave them the "help" that he did. Getting that exact same bits of information would have taken months inside the department.

Now they were going to have some sort of answers to a few questions in just a couple of days. Amazing.

Fawn just sat staring at her phone on the table between them. Then she looked up at Halligan.

"Hate to admit it, but we really did need help," she said.

"I won't tell anyone if you don't."

"Deal," she said, laughing.

CHAPTER SEVEN

February 22nd, 2019
Henderson, Nevada

Halligan had gone through both his cups of coffee and Fawn had gotten a second by the time they made it through the file, double checking everything, every detail right down to verifying times and location of where Sandy's car was found and the condition it was in. Then they had gone through the financial records that Jacob had sent them.

From what Fawn could tell, Sandy's home and auto payments had been automatically deducted from her main account until it started to get low after a year. Then someone, more than likely Reese, moved money from the savings account. That covered the payments for most of another year. Then there were a few more deposits and the payments stopped and a year later the account was closed.

They had notes to ask Reese about that.

Finally, they both felt like they had done what they could, so Fawn called Reese, using the number that Jacob had given them.

Reese answered and said she would be happy to talk with them. She remembered them both.

So at a little before four in the afternoon, Halligan and Fawn pulled up in front of a large, standard-looking suburban home not more than a thousand yards from Halligan's home and one subdivision over.

Everything in this area of Henderson was upscale and in gated subdivisions that gave the residents a sense of security without actually adding anything real.

Fawn hated the gated subdivisions because it often caused more trouble than anything with emergency response vehicles not being able to get in. And it often gave residents a feeling of security, so they dropped their guard and became easy targets for all sorts of robberies and worse.

Fawn actually felt a little nervous talking with Reese again after all these years. Especially since they didn't really have any news.

They climbed out into the now warm air of the winter after-noon. The sky was the standard bright, clear blue of Vegas, and there was very little noise at all from around the neighborhood. In fact, it actually felt a little creepy, it was so quiet.

A thin woman in running clothes opened the door as they went up the sidewalk between front areas of yard that were desert landscaped to save water. Rocks, a few desert flowers, and a few decorative cactus. Fawn bet anything that there was a small patch of grass in the backyard beside a pool. Pretty stan-dard for the mini-mansions in this area.

It took a moment for Fawn to recognize Reese. That last time she had seen her, Reese had been twenty-four and working on a master's degree at UNLV. At that point Reese had really long hair and a stressed look on her face that seemed to have set in. Sandy had disappeared when Reese was nineteen.

Those five years had to have been tough, since her parents were also dead and had left neither sister any money at all. In fact, Reese and Sandy had shouldered some of their parents' bills as well. Sandy had just got them clear of those and on top when she vanished, leaving Reese alone to deal with a missing sister.

Now the woman in front of them, smiling, was almost forty, very much in shape, with short brown hair and a tattoo on her right wrist of an eagle. She actually had no worry lines on her face that Fawn could see. To say the least, the last fifteen years had clearly been good for Reese. Married, two kids, a major college degree, and a nice house in a gated community. From where Reese had been at with her sister's disappearance, where she stood now had been a steep climb.

"Detectives Halligan and Fawn," she said, smiling and holding open her front door. Please pardon my running clothes. Just finished my daily miles when you called."

"Just glad we could talk with you again," Halligan said.

The inside of the home had a modern open floor plan and from the front door Fawn could see all the way out the kitchen patio door to the bright blue pool and green yard beyond. A tall wooden fence blocked any sign of the neighbors.

The large room was comfortable, with green-toned living room couches and chairs to one side. They did not look used much at all. Fawn bet there was a family room with a large screen television in the back somewhere.

A formal dining area with a large table sat behind the living room and also didn't look much used.

The kitchen table in front of the sliding door and the counter dividing that area from the kitchen itself was clearly used and that was where Reese led them, indicating they should sit at the dining room table.

"Anything to drink?" she asked them as she picked up what looked to be a running water bottle.

They both declined, so Reese joined them at the table, her back to the sliding door and pool beyond, her hands holding the water bottle.

Fawn decided to take the lead. "Not sure if you have heard of a cold case task force called The Cold Poker Gang?"

Reese nodded. "Retired detectives solving cold cases, right? I read about it a few times."

"Well," Halligan said, "we are both now retired and part of that task force and we are looking into your sister's disappearance with new, modern tools. See what we can find."

"Modern tools?" Reese asked, frowning.

"DNA to start with," Fawn said. "If you wouldn't mind, we would like to get a sample of your DNA and see if we can find a familial match somewhere that might lead us to Sandy."

Reese nodded. "No problem at all. That would be great. Something that couldn't be done twenty years ago."

"And we have some experts in computer searches to find patterns," Halligan said.

"You mean others might have disappeared like Sandy?" Reese asked.

"We honestly don't know," Fawn said, but she noticed that Halligan took out his notebook and wrote that down. Neither of them had thought of that possibility, but Fawn had a hunch Jacob could do the searches to find out.

After that they had decided to confirm a few details from the files again.

"Did Sandy have a boyfriend?" Fawn asked.

Reese shook her head. "No. And I tried a bunch of times to

set her up, but she just ignored me. Said she was too busy for a boyfriend. We argued a few times about that. Just stupid now in hindsight."

"So we've looked through Sandy's bank records," Halligan said. "Could you describe what happened there?"

Reese went on to describe exactly what both Fawn and Halligan had guessed had happened from their look at the records.

So with a few more questions to confirm a few more details that were in the file like where the car was found and what Reese had done with it years later, they thanked her and stood.

Fawn took out the DNA gathering kit that Halligan had in his car and got a swab from Reese; then they headed for the front door.

"Promise to keep me informed if you learn anything at all," Reese said, as they went back into the afternoon sun.

"We will," Fawn said. "Don't get your hopes up. Seventeen years is a long time."

"But at least you are trying," Reese said. "And that means everything to me."

"To us as well," Halligan said. "I never forgot about your sister."

"Neither did I," Fawn said.

"Thank you," Reese said as they headed down the sidewalk.

And Fawn had zero doubt that Reese meant that.

CHAPTER EIGHT

February 22nd, 2019
Henderson, Nevada

Halligan got the car turned around and headed back toward the entrance gate of the subdivision as Fawn pulled out her phone and called Jacob.

She put the phone on speaker and held it between them, since they had forgotten to hook her phone into the dashboard of the car.

"Got us both," she said when Jacob answered. "We got the DNA sample from Sandy's sister. Where should we take it or send it?"

"Judy and I are headed to her grandfather's house. You want to meet us there?"

Fawn glanced at Halligan and he nodded. He would love to see Young again.

"Perfect," Fawn said. "We'll be there in about ten minutes."

"Also," Halligan said, "got another idea."

He decided to tell Jacob the idea that Reese had had about others being taken. No way seventeen years ago he could have done that kind of search with any wide base. Just not possible, but now he had a hunch it was very possible.

"Could you set up a search through the records of other women around Sandy's age vanishing like she did? See if there were others, if this was a pattern of some sort."

Fawn was nodding beside him and added nothing to the question.

"Sure," Jacob said. "Judy will start it now as we head to Young's place. See you there."

With that he hung up and Fawn put her phone back in her jacket pocket, shaking her head.

Halligan felt sort of amazed. "You ever get the feeling that the world sort of went by us in the last ten years?"

"Getting it," Fawn said. "Just wondering why they don't assign a computer geek with clearance to every active detective. A ton more stuff would get done and solved."

"Paperwork," Halligan said, trying not to shudder. "Remember that? The poor computer person would have to track every detail."

"Oh, yeah," she said, laughing to herself. "I sort of forgot we are free of all that."

"Oh, I'm never forgetting. I wouldn't be here if we had to do paperwork for all this."

Fawn laughed, then said, "I wouldn't either, and then I would be missing the fun of being driven all over the city."

"You said I didn't suck," Halligan said, laughing. "So now I'm good enough to be a chauffeur?"

"Oh, I wouldn't go that far," Fawn said.

"One spoiled cop," Halligan said, smiling at her. "So exactly how far would you go?"

"A woman never tells," she said, smiling back.

Halligan just shook his head and pretended to concentrate on his driving.

Damn, first day and he was already having more fun being partners with Fawn than he had had in years. That was a very, very good sign for the future.

CHAPTER NINE

February 22nd, 2019
Henderson, Nevada

Fawn and Halligan clearly arrived at Young's home after Jacob and Judy, since Jacob's car was in the driveway.

Young's home was a nice but older three-bedroom in what used to be an upscale subdivision in the 1980s, but now with all the mini-mansion subdivisions in the Henderson area, it looked like a regular home for regular people. It even had a small green front yard that Fawn bet Young paid extra in water costs to maintain. Or more than likely in the summer he just let it go brown.

Young answered the front door with a grin on his face and gave Fawn a huge hug, then did the same to Halligan. Fawn was surprised that Halligan was a hugger, but he clearly was with the right people, and Young was one of the right people.

Retired Metro Officer Matthew Young might be the most universally liked officer on the force. A number of times he could have moved to detective, but just said he enjoyed patrol and wanted to stay there. Then his wife Barbara had gotten sick and a year before she died, he had retired to be with her.

Andor had been trying to get him into the task force for a while now.

Young didn't look his almost seventy years, that was for sure. He carried himself ramrod straight and had a full head of thick, gray hair. His eyes always seemed to be laughing or smiling at something. Clearly the zest for life now kept him young.

Fawn knew he had two daughters and a bunch of grandkids. And one of those grandkids who dressed like Jacob had her head buried in a laptop next to Jacob, who was on another laptop on the couch. The picture of young love these days from what Fawn could tell. Although, after the last ten years, eight of them with "the cheating bastard" and two alone, she had no idea what love might even be like.

Jacob said, without looking up from the computer, "Put the swab on my backpack near the door."

Halligan smiled at Fawn and did as he was told. Then Young indicated that they should let the kids work and the three of them went into the kitchen to grab some water and catch up.

Young was glad to hear that the two of them retired and were teamed up. "You two always fit together in my mind."

"Only one day so far and neither of us are dead," Halligan said. "And she said I didn't suck as a driver."

"Wow," Young said. "High praise from Fawn here. And on the first day."

Fawn laughed. "I knew I was going to regret saying that."

"So I heard," Halligan said to Young, "that you were thinking of selling and downsizing some."

"I was," Young said. "Both my daughters thought it would be good for me since for most of the last two years I just sort of rattled around in this place since Barbara died. But now I'm back keeping it up and taking care of myself, so I think I'm going to stay. Kind of like the memories."

Halligan nodded. "I think I need to make some new memories these days and my place is so huge I got to get out of it."

"I really do need new memories as well," Fawn said.

Young laughed. "You ever shoot the balls off that cheating bastard of a husband?"

Fawn shook her head. "Thought about it a bunch of times, but inflicted more pain in the divorce two years ago."

"That a girl," Young said, patting her arm.

"And thanks for the help on all that," Fawn said. Young had helped her track the bastard a few times, doing a little off-the-books undercover work for her.

"My pleasure," Young said.

"Oh, I sense a story there," Halligan said.

"Remember I said a girl never tells," Fawn said, smiling at her partner.

"Damn," Halligan said.

Young thought that wonderfully funny.

At that point Jacob yelled from the living room. "Hey guys, I think we might have something here."

Fawn didn't think she had seen three old cops move so fast before, at least not without a gun aimed at them.

CHAPTER TEN

February 22nd, 2019
Henderson, Nevada

Halligan stood across from Jacob and Judy who were sitting on Young's brown cloth couch. Both were still staring at their laptops, their fingers seeming to move like magic over the keys. Halligan had never got much past the hunt and peck system of typing, so anyone who could do what they were doing always impressed him.

The three stood there silently for what seemed like a long time, but was actually only about thirty seconds before Jacob looked up.

"Grandpa," Judy said, "We're using your printer to print out this list."

"And I have downloaded the list to both of your phones," Jacob said to Fawn and Halligan.

"A list of what?" Fawn asked.

Halligan had a sinking feeling he knew of what.

"We have found thirty-two other women about Sandy's age when she vanished who also vanished in the same fashion over a ten-year period starting from 1999 through 2009 here in Las Vegas. Eleven years."

"All are active missing persons' cases," Judy said.

"Thirty-three total missing women?" Fawn said, softly.

"Well, shit," Young said. "How in the hell did someone not put that together?"

"They were spread evenly every year," Jacob said. "Always one in March, another in August, another in November. Eleven years the pattern went on until it suddenly stopped in November of 2009, eleven years after the first one. So good idea having us search for this."

"Got the idea from Sandy's sister," Halligan said.

He was having trouble wrapping his mind around thirty-three missing women, vanishing in the same fashion as Sandy. That meant 32 more families out there wondering what happened, just as Reese had done for twenty-one years.

"I just sent the list to Andor to request copies of all the files of those cases," Jacob said. "My hunch is that it will take until tomorrow morning before you get them."

"In the meantime," Judy said, "we'll run programs to figure out similarities of all the women. Age, height, hair color. We do know that all were single. And all worked on the Strip in some hotel or casino or another."

"Family history as well," Fawn said.

Halligan nodded to that, as did Jacob and Judy. Clearly Fawn was grasping this a little quicker than he was.

"Add in car abandoned locations if they had cars," Halligan said.

At that moment Halligan's phone buzzed and he glanced down at it.

"Andor," Halligan said, shaking his head and clicking it on.

"You got me, Fawn, Young, Judy, and Jacob all on speaker phone. Seems there is a little bit more to this dead-end case you gave us."

"You think?" Andor said, his voice gruff. "I got all the files being fast-tracked to have them to you in about an hour. You'll have to come back downtown to pick them up."

"Thanks," Halligan said.

"Don't thank me," Andor said. "Chief is the one who put a rush on this. Thirty-three women missing and we didn't catch the pattern. Makes the department look bad. Meet you in one hour out front of the main building."

With that Andor hung up.

Young turned and headed for his office to get the printout.

"How did we miss it?" Halligan asked, more to himself as he clicked off his phone.

"Five to seven people a day go missing in this town and have reports filed," Jacob said without looking up. "That's not per week, that's every day. Over two hundred per month. And again, those are just the ones that reports are filed on. Not telling how many missing persons every day go unreported."

"And most show up after a few days," Judy said, "but a lot of them go missing because they are escaping something and don't want to be found."

"Police have little they can do unless it is clear a crime is involved with a person vanishing," Jacob said. "You both did as much as you could on the Goodson case with no clear evidence of a crime."

Halligan nodded. He knew all that. But it still felt like he might have missed something. He was good at blaming himself for the few cases he couldn't solve over the years.

"I know a few of these cases," Young said, coming back into the room while scanning the pages.

"Hang on," Judy said. "I think I may have just found some more help."

She glanced up and Halligan could see the intelligence in her eyes, just like in Jacob's eyes.

"Three of the families over the years hired the same private investigator to look into the disappearances," Judy said. "From what I can tell, he's still working the cases all these years later."

Halligan nodded. Often private investigators were hired by families to find someone. The problem is that if the missing person doesn't want to be found and the PI finds them, the PI is barred by pretty stiff laws from revealing the location of the person, without the missing person's permission. Puts the PI in tough spots at times.

And some PIs are great, some not so much.

"Who is it?" Fawn asked.

"Brian Newport," Judy said.

"He's one of the good ones," Young said.

All Fawn and Halligan could do was nod.

Halligan knew Brian, had worked with him on a couple of cases. Brian was ex-government and knew the law. A careful investigator who often helped the police more than his clients when he stumbled across something.

It looked like their case with very few leads had suddenly blown sky high. He and Fawn had some long nights ahead of them, that was for sure.

And he honestly wasn't going to mind that in the slightest. Especially if they could solve this and give answers to all those families.

CHAPTER ELEVEN

February 22nd, 2019
Las Vegas, Nevada

Fawn was amused that it took the two of them almost a full five minutes to figure out the traffic maps on the screen on Halligan's new Cadillac. Jacob or Judy would have done it in a few seconds, she was sure. Thankfully, with her using the manual in the glove box, they got it worked out and discovered the main freeway headed downtown was at a full stop.

So Halligan now had them on the Maryland Parkway, headed toward the downtown area and she was thumbing through the printout of all the missing women's names.

Just as Young had said, she recognized a few of the women's names and had actually been lead detective on one of the cases for a short time back in 2008. She doubted that without Jacob's and Judy's help she ever would have connected that case and the Goodson case. Just no surface reason to.

"So how do you want to approach Brian?" Halligan asked.

"Thinking we just call him, tell him what we are doing and what we have found so far and ask him if he would be willing to share what he has found on his three cases."

Fawn had worked twice with Brian and she liked him. And she liked his wife. By now, his two boys would be grown and more than likely in college. She was actually partially surprised he was still working.

"Sounds like as good a plan as any," Halligan said. "Going to take us another 15 minutes to get downtown in this traffic. Might as well do it now."

Fawn grabbed the car manual out of the glove box and quickly looked up how to put her phone into the car system, then did so, then dialed Brian's number that Jacob had given them.

Brian's voice came strongly through the car speakers. "Detective Fawn," he said. "What a pleasant surprise."

"Thanks, Brian," she said. "Great hearing your voice again. I'm here in Detective Halligan's car and we're on speaker phone."

"Halligan," Brian said, laughing, "I am amazed you are working with anyone."

"We're both retired now, actually," Halligan said.

"Oh, don't tell me, Andor put you together on the cold case task force?"

"He did," Fawn said, "But we requested it."

"Now you are just hurting my head," Brian said. "But I suppose you didn't call after all these years just to give me a headache. So what's up?"

"We are working a twenty-year-old missing person's case," Fawn said.

"Andor's handing out the easy cases these days, huh?" Brain said and then laughed.

"Well, it looked impossible until a couple of computer geeks we have helping us discovered a pattern in other missing person's cases. Thirty-three women, to be exact, three per year for eleven years up until 2009."

"Oh, shit," Brian said. "Thirty-three? Damn it all to hell. And I bet I got three of them, right?"

"You do," Fawn said.

"I always thought those three cases were too damn similar. Just never could get my fingers on an edge to dig in."

"You mind sharing your information on them and we'll keep you informed from our side on what we find as well?" Fawn asked.

"Absolutely," Brian said. "And if you need extra help, I'm all in. I've been keeping those three cases active for all these years for the families without charge because I just couldn't let the cases go. They ate at me."

"Both Halligan and I took runs at the case Andor gave us when it was still active and it ate at both of us as well. Just the nature of how the women all vanished without a trace."

"Exactly," Brian said. "Where you at now?"

"Headed to the main precinct downtown to get copies of all thirty-three files," Fawn said.

"My office is over on 8th near Bonneville, tucked in with all the lawyers' offices," Brian said. "Give me an hour and I'll have copies of all my files for you as well."

"Thank you," Fawn said. "We'll stop by."

"No, thank you both. If you can make progress on these cases, you will save me some future sleepless nights. And help a lot of families."

"Exactly," Fawn said. "See you shortly."

With that she hung up and glanced at Halligan who was nodding.

"Seems we are building a good team on this one," Fawn said.

"Now we just have to solve it."

Fawn nodded. "Yeah, there is always that."

CHAPTER TWELVE

February 22nd, 2019
Las Vegas, Nevada

Andor was standing in front of the big four-story office building that contained the main Metro headquarters. He was leaning against four file boxes. Luckily the winter day was nice, no real wind, and slightly warm.

"He got all that copied in an hour?" Halligan said, feeling surprised. "He must have had an army in there helping him."

"When the Chief wants something done," Fawn said.

Halligan could only nod to that.

Halligan pulled up so that they could load the boxes into the back of the SUV.

"Thanks," Halligan said to Andor when they got them loaded. "We got Brian Newport getting us his files on three of the women he got hired to find."

Andor nodded. "Brian's a good one. He will help you if you need it. Don't hesitate in using him."

"He offered," Fawn said.

"If you need an active on this, call Detective Little," Andor said. "I got him up to speed as much as I could."

Halligan knew Martin Little and liked him a lot. Tall guy, used to play semi-pro basketball before joining Metro. A force of nature, but with a great personality that blunted the roughness.

"Marty gets all this paperwork, huh?" Fawn asked, shaking her head.

"Only if you solve this mess," Andor said.

"Not if," Fawn said. "When."

"I'll warn Marty you said that," Andor said. Then he turned and headed back inside without even saying goodbye.

Ten minutes later, Halligan had his car parked in front of what had been a standard 1930s Tutor-style home at one point, but had now been remodeled into a very nice professional-looking office with Brian's name on a wooden sign near the sidewalk. The old oak and maple trees that lined both sides of the street and in most of the yards, gave the street a real professional feel.

Every old home along the road had been remodeled into a professional office, almost all lawyers' offices since the courthouse was only three blocks away.

Blocks and blocks of the old downtown Las Vegas now looked exactly like this road with some new modern construction scattered among the remodels.

If Halligan had to bet, the average cost of one of these older homes on this street far surpassed the cost of the mini-mansions out in Henderson like his place.

Brian opened the door for them as they came up the sidewalk and brought out a bankers file box.

Brian looked pretty much as Halligan remembered him from the last time they met on a case about ten years before. Brian had a full head of gray hair that seemed to always be uncombed. He was medium height and had a good-sized stomach on him. He had on a button-up blue golf sweater and matching blue slacks and tennis shoes.

He put down the box and gave Fawn a hug, then shook Halligan's hand.

"Man am I glad you two are taking a run at this," Brian said. "Thought I was going to go to my grave with these three cases unsolved."

"You're not out of this yet," Fawn said.

"And we might need your help if this shapes up to be as strange and as bad as it looks," Halligan said.

"Anything except trying to run down a bad guy on foot," Brian said, patting his stomach.

All three laughed, then Brian picked up the box and handed it to Halligan. "You would think that with all the work I did on these three cases I would have more than this."

"Whoever took these women was a real pro," Fawn said. "And covered their tracks very well."

"But in thirty-three women over ten years," Halligan said, "we're betting that person or persons slipped somewhere."

"I'm betting you are right," Brian said, nodding. "But one question has me stumped since you called. You said the cases seemed to vanish in 2009. Got a hunch if you got some computer help, the reason for that stopping might be a way to come at this from the outside."

Halligan nodded.

"We'll get them working that angle," Fawn said. "It's only been a few hours since we discovered all this."

Halligan suddenly had an idea. "Let me put this in the car and let you take a look at a printout of all thirty cases we know about so far."

He turned and put the box in the back with the others from Andor, then got the printout and handed it to Brian.

Fawn and Halligan stood quietly in the late afternoon cool air, watching as Brian leafed through the names. He nodded a couple of times.

"My three are on here and I might recognize a couple of the other names as well. Mind if I make a copy of this?"

"Sure," Fawn said after Halligan nodded.

Brian ducked back inside his office.

"I know we don't have any more real leads than we had when we started today," Fawn said. "And the case has gotten a ton bigger. But I feel like we have a chance with Jacob, Judy, Young, and now Brian helping us."

"I agree," Halligan said. "And this is a ton better than you holding down a perp and me making them drink a truth drug."

"Nope, you're doing the holding, remember," Fawn said, trying to keep a straight face, but without luck. "Besides, Andor hasn't given us any of the secret drugs yet."

"You get to ask him," Halligan said.

With that Fawn just started laughing.

Halligan had to admit, the idea of asking Andor for a mythical truth drug was funny.

CHAPTER THIRTEEN

February 22nd, 2019
Henderson, Nevada

Fawn sat comfortably in the passenger seat as Halligan got them back out of downtown Las Vegas and headed back to Henderson. It was just after five in the evening and the traffic was normally bad, so it took them almost thirty minutes on ground streets, staying off the jammed freeways.

On the way out, they had decided to work at Halligan's place, since he had a large unused dining room table and a bunch of empty spare bedrooms to store the boxes in. That beat her condo that was barely large enough for her to spread out in, let along put files on thirty different cases in any kind of order.

"Been a long first day, hasn't it?" Halligan said.

Fawn nodded in agreement. "And we seemed to have skipped lunch."

"Was thinking just that. How about we drop the boxes at my

place and then get some sushi. If you like sushi, there is a small place close to my house that I am a regular at."

"I love sushi," she said, glad that Halligan did as well. "I usually go to a place out Eastern."

"You'll love this place, then," he said.

Five minutes later he got them through the front gate of the subdivision he lived in and after two turns, both left, both first streets to the left, he pulled up in front of a home that looked like most of the other homes in the subdivision. And Fawn knew that was on purpose. Individuality did not mix with the idea of a homeowner's association.

The house from the outside even looked huge and the lots the homes sat on in this subdivision were larger than she had seen before, with actual room between the homes. The land-scaping was all desert, done to look like the rest of the homes. Nothing about this place felt like Halligan.

"I have got to get out of this place sooner rather than later," Halligan said, pulling up into the driveway and shutting down the car. "This was Cindy's dream home and we never really got a chance to enjoy it with her cancer."

"Moving is a lot of work," Fawn said.

"Got to do it," Halligan said. "And I honestly have very little that I would need to take with me. You'll see. Place echoes it's so empty."

As they climbed out into the quickly cooling air as the sun was starting to go down, Fawn asked. "What kind of place are you looking for?"

Halligan smiled. "And that's the problem and exactly why I am still here."

He headed for the front door to unlock it and turn off the alarm, then came back. "Dining room is just to the inside on the right of the front door. Step down so watch out for the step."

They both grabbed just one box, since the boxes were amazingly heavy stuffed with so much paper.

The inside of the house had the same modern look as the outside, and Halligan hadn't been exaggerating when he said it echoed. Their footsteps actually did from the high ceilings and eggshell white walls and tile floors. This house would need a lot of art on the walls, soft cloth furniture, and throw rugs to warm it up.

The furniture in the main living room to the left of the front door might as well still have the plastic coverings, it all looked so new and unused. And Fawn had no doubt that the brand new huge dark-oak dining room table that filled the formal dining room was about to be used for the first time, just not for its intended purpose.

Cindy had been dead for three years, Fawn knew that. And clearly in this part of the house, Halligan had never lived.

They put the boxes on the table, then headed back for the car. "How soon after you bought this place did Cindy get sick?" Fawn asked.

"She was diagnosed just two weeks after we bought the place," Halligan said. "I live in the kitchen with the table there, in the family room with the television, and what was a guest bedroom suite off the family room. Mudroom right from the garage."

"When was the last time before now that you had opened the front door?" Fawn asked as they both grabbed another box.

"Before Cindy died."

Fawn just shook her head. "Yup, you got to get out of this place. It's time. Let some family enjoy it."

"No doubt about that," he said.

"I'll be glad to help."

He glanced over at her and she could tell her offer meant a lot to him.

"Thank you," he said.

He led the way back into the house and at that moment, as she watched him walk, she realized just how much she cared about him, not only as a friend, but maybe a little bit more.

Maybe. She would have to think about that. She had known him so long, the friendship covered a lot.

But first things first, they had thirty-three missing persons cases to solve. And not one clue how to go about it.

CHAPTER FOURTEEN

February 22nd, 2019
Henderson, Nevada

It had been slightly embarrassing for Halligan to show Fawn his house. Granted, he had kept it up, and it was worth more than a million and was paid off, but letting her see how he had lived for the last three years just sort of shone a spotlight on his problem of not moving on after he had lost Cindy.

He hadn't wanted to move on at first. He had decided to give himself time. Everyone told him that was healthy. But retiring now and joining the task force and working with Fawn made it clear it had become time. Past time, actually. He realized with showing Fawn the big empty house that even Cindy would be disgusted with him.

And Fawn's offer to help meant a lot to him. That alone might be enough to get him going. He just needed to figure out where.

The sushi place with the name he could never pronounce

was tucked to one end of an older strip mall. It clearly had existed in this location for a very long time.

The décor was dark and cramped. The booths had tall backs and curtains and were spaced along one wall. A sushi bar fit along part of the other side and the back wall with six chairs. Maybe totally full the place could hold forty people. He had never seen it full, but he had also never seen it empty.

There were two other couples, both sitting at the bar with two chairs between them when he and Fawn entered.

The owner, a small wrinkled Asian woman who didn't seem to speak English but understood it perfectly waved at him from the back and he pointed to the booth near the door and she nodded.

Both he and Fawn had their notebooks, but first he handed Fawn a plastic coated long card that was the menu from where they were stashed against the wall and then took another for himself.

"Everything I have tried is great," he said.

"What have you tried?" Fawn asked, staring at the menu that's only value was the pictures unless you could read Japanese.

He held up the entire menu and she laughed.

They both studied the menus and Halligan realized he was really hungry. He was going to over order and he didn't care.

When the owner appeared beside their booth, paper and pen in her hand, and bowed slightly without saying a word, they both pointed to the pictures of what they wanted, both ordered tea and white rice as well.

She again bowed slightly and left. Not a word was said.

Fawn just looked around and smiled. "This place is great and I see why you like it. You don't have to talk to anyone."

"Food's good too," he said, smiling.

"Just a bonus," she said, smiling at him. Then she took out her notebook and opened it.

He did the same, then said, "We need to brainstorm any possible opening into this mess."

"Agreed," she said. "Brian's suggestion of studying what might have caused this to stop is a good one."

Halligan nodded and started writing. "A sex ring busted, someone arrested and jailed for attempted kidnapping and so on."

"Death of a known sex offender," Fawn said.

They both wrote for a bit, then stopped.

"We have Jacob and Judy searching patterns in all the victims," Fawn said.

"That might crack something," Halligan said. "We know they all worked on the Strip, so maybe there's a way that someone there got all their private information."

"Jacob could find that I'm sure," Fawn said.

"How about the first one that we know about," Halligan said. "Something in her family or past."

Fawn nodded. "Something started all this. Exactly."

They both wrote for a minute, then Fawn looked up at Halligan. "Why the exact pattern of when they were taken? Did it take time to get rid of each one, or kill each one, or dispose of the bodies before taking another?"

"A bunch of possible hand-holds there," Halligan said. "But thirty-three women. If they are dead, that's thirty-three bodies to dispose of. If they are still alive, where would they be after all this time?"

"So we search for ways to dispose of bodies without anyone noticing, or the person fakes records for the disposing of the bodies."

Suddenly Halligan had a very, very difficult question that sort of knocked him back on his seat.

"What?" Fawn asked, seeing his reaction.

"Sandy Goodson was driving on her way to work. She never made the employee parking garage. Right?"

"That's what the report said and got a hunch we both double-checked that way back. I know I did," Fawn said.

Halligan nodded. "How did someone get in the car with her? I always thought she was carjacked or something, but if that was the case, in thirty-three women, one or two would have gotten away."

"And there would be witnesses," Fawn said. "Those are all main streets that at least Sandy would have been traveling."

"So why would Sandy pull over and let another person into her car?"

"A woman," Fawn said. "In some sort of trouble and wearing gloves since we never found a trace of anyone else ever being in the car with her."

Halligan nodded. "And most likely wearing the same hotel uniform that she was wearing."

Fawn sat back, just sort of staring into the distance.

Halligan felt the same way. They had found a critical detail they never would have thought about without there being so many women who were missing.

At that moment the sushi came and it took a moment for Halligan to remember how hungry he was and that he really needed to eat.

CHAPTER FIFTEEN

February 22nd, 2019
Henderson, Nevada

Fawn couldn't believe it was only seven in the evening when they finished dinner. This might have been one of the longest days she could remember. And over the years she had had a lot of long days.

But spending it with Halligan had made the long day and all the information a pleasure.

They both agreed that how the women got stopped was a critical element to solving all these, so they decided that after dinner they would call Jacob and see if he could find any information from that angle. If there was some employee in common working with all the missing women.

And chances are the woman would have changed her name, so they needed to ask if a search of employee records from the hotels from back then included pictures. They were both sure it had.

But chances are it was just a woman who somehow managed to get hold of employee uniforms. If that was the case, this would be a dead end.

But then the question was could it really be a woman? A woman working solo or with others to abduct other women.

The food gave Fawn some energy and Halligan had been right, it was amazing. Maybe the best sushi in Henderson.

The older woman waved goodbye to them as they headed out the door and climbed into Halligan's Cadillac. Fawn used her phone to call Jacob as Halligan started up the car.

"Detective Fawn," Jacob said.

"I'm here with Halligan on speaker phone," she said. "We've got a couple of ideas to run past you."

"Fire," Jacob said. "Judy is here with me."

"We believe that the only way these women would have stopped on the way to work on a busy street for a stranger is that if that stranger was a woman and seemed to be in trouble and maybe even was wearing the same hotel uniform as the victim."

Silence for a moment on the other end, then Jacob said, "Of course. "You think it might be another employee of the hotel at the time?"

"It might have been," Halligan said. "It would make sense that the victim's information and address could be gotten by another employee."

"Or that the victim even knew the woman abducting them," Fawn said. "Can you get into those hotel records from those ten years?"

Silence for a moment, then Jacob came back. "Let us put together a quick date of when each woman worked at each hotel, see if we can see a pattern, then we should know if there is overlap and which hotels to get the records from. I'll call you right back."

With that he clicked off and Fawn looked at Halligan. "You think we might have something?"

"I do," he said, nodding. With that he put the car in gear and went to pull out of the small lot.

"Where are we headed?" Fawn asked, putting on her seat belt.

"Dessert," Halligan said. "You want to split a Cinnaholic cinnamon roll with me?"

"Damned straight," she said, laughing. "Love those things. Sinful. Not even possible that they are vegan."

"I agree," he said, expertly taking them out onto the road and turning right to go the three blocks to where the most amazing cinnamon rolls on the planet lived.

She usually tried to avoid the place, but at least twice a month failed and ended up with a number of cinnamon rolls in her fridge that somehow, with intense discipline, took her a few days to eat.

"You ever surprised at how much alike we are?" Fawn asked.

"Been surprising me all day," he said. "And I've been enjoying the hell out of it."

"Me too," she said. "Me too."

Twenty minutes later, they had just finished off the warm cinnamon roll and were sitting in the car in the mall parking lot where the shop was at when Jacob called back.

"Good thinking, Detectives," Jacob said. "Every year the three women who went missing all worked at the same casino. In different jobs, in different areas of the casinos. But for five years running, every woman who went missing worked at an MGM Grand corporation property, including Sandy Goodson who was fairly new working at the Luxor."

"So someone in the HR department might be our abductor," Halligan said.

"For two years running the six women taken worked at a Wynn Property," Jacob said. "So we got into the employment records of both corporations and the only woman who worked at both places during those years was a woman by the name of Angel Bocci. She had a flawless record and was promoted a number of times over the years."

"You getting a warrant for those searches?" Fawn asked, glancing at Halligan.

"In the process," Jacob said. "We'll do an official, under-warrant search in the morning. Just thought we would get a slight jump because there is a chance the warrant might tip someone off. With thirty-three women, no telling how deep this goes."

"Great thinking," Halligan said and Fawn agreed.

"Is she still around town?"

"Went missing around Christmas of 2009," Jacob said. "We'll see who and what we can find about that."

Fawn nodded. "Right when the disappearance stopped. Well that answered that question."

"At least they stopped here," Jacob said. "We're going to run searches for the same patterns after 2009 in both Reno and Atlantic City."

"Fantastic," Halligan said.

Fawn just sort of shuddered at the idea there might be more than thirty-three women lost in this mess.

"I'll contact you in the morning," Jacob said, "with more information we get from the warrant. And possible contacts. Tonight Judy and I are going to search for trackers, someone watching out for activity on this case."

"Thank you," Fawn said.

And with that, Jacob clicked off.

Halligan had a serious and worried look on his face. "Jacob thinks we might just have our hands in a hornet's nest."

Fawn nodded. "The deeper we get into this, the more I am worried about the exact same thing."

CHAPTER SIXTEEN

February 23rd, 2019
Henderson, Nevada

It was barely eight in the morning when Halligan pulled into a parking space in front of Fawn's condo complex and she came out. She had on a light jacket, a white blouse underneath, jeans and running shoes. She looked freshly showered and was smiling.

He knew that she had already been out for a 5k run and now they were headed for a breakfast spot about four blocks away. She looked amazingly attractive and full of life.

He had on a light blue jacket that covered his badge and gun, jeans, and a dress shirt with the sleeves rolled up. He also wore running shoes, but not because he was a runner like Fawn. They were just comfortable on long days like yesterday.

After they had finished talking with Jacob last night, they had gone back to Halligan's big empty house and worked for three hours on the files, just seeing if there was anything they could find in the investigations. They had found a few small things, but nothing they would chase unless this lead with Angel Bocci completely went cold.

What was even more amazing was how thin all those files were. Missing person's cases could only be taken so far by the police if there was no positive crime involved. And not one of these had an obvious crime that they could see, other than all 33 women had gone missing in the same fashion.

Halligan had taken Fawn home at a little after ten and they had agreed to meet at eight for breakfast. Eggs and waffles would be much better than his normal two protein bars he managed to wash down with coffee every morning.

He really, really needed to change his life, get out of that house, start to move on again before he was too old to do so. He knew that was a silly thought, since he was only 55, but it was the one that kept coming up over and over. And when that happened, he needed to listen and make the changes.

The breakfast restaurant they both liked was off of Eastern and tucked a ways back from the road in what seemed to be more office than retail shops. It looked more like a Denny's than anything, with plastic booths with high backs for privacy and a long counter with stools, but Halligan knew it was privately owned and this one location was the only one.

From five in the morning until after lunch, the place always seemed busy and the wait staff always friendly.

And the breakfasts were great. Large portions, always perfectly done. Halligan ordered a three-egg ham and bacon omelet with toast and a side of strawberries. Fawn ordered three eggs over medium with toast and regular fruit cup. They both ordered coffee as well and the owner stopped by after a moment to say good morning with a full pot and just set it on the table.

"You think he knows us?" Halligan asked, shaking his head as he poured them both a cup.

"Just saving his staff time trying to keep our cups full," Fawn said. "Smart business."

For the next ten minutes while they waited for food, Fawn quizzed him on where he wanted to live in the valley, what kind of place would make him feel like home, and what size.

Halligan was surprised that he knew some of the answers. "Not a subdivision." And then in response to the size question he said, "Two bedroom."

Where in the valley he wanted to live was a more difficult question. He liked Henderson mostly because he knew where everything was. He wouldn't want to live downtown because, for one thing, it had a lot of tourists along Fremont Street. And it was a grocery store desert. He really loved the upscale stores in Henderson. And both the North side of town and Summerlin didn't interest him at all.

"So you clearly want to stay in town," Fawn asked, smiling. "Not move out into the desert somewhere?"

He laughed. "Oh, not a chance."

"So not a subdivision," Fawn said, "but in Henderson, the home of subdivisions. You like doing yard work?"

"Nope," Halligan said. "I hire a company to take care of my yard."

Fawn smiled. "Sounds to me like you are headed to a condo. Let me show you my place and see what you think when we get a break."

"Thank you," Halligan said. "Really appreciate the help."

At that moment the food came and they got halfway through their breakfasts when Jacob called.

Fawn glanced around to see if any other customers were close enough to hear, then put the call on speaker.

"Morning Jacob," she said. "Hope you two got a little sleep."

"A little," Jacob said. "As far as we can tell, this entire thing stopped with the last woman in 2009. Nothing similar in Reno, Atlantic City, or anywhere else that popped up in our searches."

"That's a relief," Fawn said.

Halligan felt himself relax a little with that.

"And as far as we can tell," Jacob said, "there is no monitoring going on of any of this at all. And yesterday when the Chief and Andor got those files for us, they didn't take any precautions and if there had been monitoring, it would have been triggered there."

"So let me get this straight," Fawn said. "These thirty-three cases don't seem to still have any ongoing oversight from whoever did it."

"Correct," Jacob said. "At least as much as we can find and we can find most anything."

Halligan nodded to that as well. Two reasons to be relieved. But that brought them back to why this was even done in the first place.

"So it seemed to end when this Angel Bocci vanished," Halligan said. "Any more information about her?"

"Fake name, fake identification, fake everything," Jacob said. "But very well done. No one would catch any of it without looking closely like we are doing. So my guess is that she really isn't missing, just went back to who she was before all this started."

"Any chance on facial recognition with her?" Fawn asked.

"Got requests into the hotels she worked at for pictures. Should have them at any moment."

"Thanks, Jacob," Halligan said. "Check in if you get anything and we'll do the same if we come up with any ideas."

"Sounds good," Jacob said and hung up.

"Well," Fawn said, putting her phone back in her pocket and going back to her unfinished breakfast. "This didn't get worse at least."

"But we got almost nothing," Halligan said, also digging back into his half-finished omelet.

"We still got thirty-three case files we need to take a closer look at," Fawn said. "And that box of information on three of them from Brian. We haven't even looked at that yet."

She was right. They actually had a lot to do.

"So back to the dining room and good old-fashioned detective work."

"You make that sound like a bad thing," Fawn said. "You do know we are old?"

"Fifty-five is not old," Halligan said, smiling.

"You're going to be old if you stay in that big house by yourself much longer."

With that he just took another bite of omelet and nodded. She was right, and he knew it.

CHAPTER SEVENTEEN

February 23rd, 2019
Henderson, Nevada

Fawn had really enjoyed breakfast with Halligan. The two of them were getting along even better than she had hoped, and working alone the last number of years had made her realize she had missed being with another person.

She just hoped Halligan was enjoying being with her as much. He sure seemed to be.

On the way to Halligan's house to get back to the task of searching through the files, Jacob sent the picture of Angel Bocci. Long black hair that looked like a wig, dark thin eyebrows and a smile that didn't reach her dark brown eyes.

"Not someone I would want to get to know," Halligan said as Fawn showed him the picture. "She seems angry."

"Yeah," Fawn said. "How old would you say she is in this picture?"

She once again held up the image on her phone for Halligan to see while they were stopped at a light.

He shrugged. "Anywhere from late 20s to 40. Too much fake to get to the real age."

She agreed with that.

"I'm going to send this to Brian and then call him and give him an update," Fawn said.

"He'll be as relieved as we are about this not going any farther. Thirty-three missing women is enough."

She sent Brian the picture, then called him.

"Who exactly is this picture of?" Brian asked when he answered.

Fawn went through how they had figured out that the only way for any of the women to stop was for another woman, wearing the same hotel uniform, pretending to be in trouble alongside the road.

"Great thinking," Brian said. "I always assumed they were carjacked or something. But that never really made sense because no trace of anyone else was ever found in the three cars I dealt with."

"The picture I sent you is of Angel Bocci," Fawn said, "who worked in all the hotels the women were working in when they vanished. Bocci vanished in 2009 after the last woman that year and was reported missing, but Jacob discovered that the Bocci name is totally fake, came into being in late 1998 just before all this started."

"Absolutely it's fake," Brian said. "This is a picture of Jean Hult with fake hair and different eyebrows. She was the first of the thirty-three women to vanish and one of the three I was hired to find by her family. Her picture is in the file. Have Jacob do a facial comparison."

"You're not kidding, are you?" Halligan said after a moment of silence in the car.

Fawn just sort of sat there, not knowing what to think.

"Not kidding in the slightest," Brian said.

Fawn took a deep breath. "We're getting images of all the women from the hotels shortly. We'll let you know what that digs up and if facial confirms that Bocci actually is Hult."

"Thanks," Brian said. "At least I will know sort of what happened to one of my clients. Sort of. This is one messed-up pile you guys are wading into. Call me if you need help. I'll drop everything."

With that he hung up.

Fawn just looked over at Halligan who was shaking his head.

Fawn called Jacob and told him what Brian said. Then, when they reached Halligan's house, the first thing they did was open up Brian's file of Jean Hult and compare the picture to the one Jacob had sent them of Bocci.

Brian was right. It was the same woman. There was no doubt in Fawn's mind.

So what in the hell had been going on with those women for ten years? And where were they now?

CHAPTER EIGHTEEN

February 23rd, 2019
Henderson, Nevada

Halligan had something bothering him, one of those thoughts that you knew was there but you couldn't pull it to the front.

It wasn't until they had coffee made and they were getting ready to start into the files when the thought finally surfaced.

"Hang on a minute," he said. "If Bocci is actually Hult, how could they both be working at the hotel at the same time?"

Fawn stared at him with those wonderful eyes of hers, then shook her head and picked up the phone.

"Detective," Jacob said when he answered. "This is one really twisted mess."

"Yeah," Fawn said, "Halligan was wondering how Bocci and Hult could both work at the same casino at the same time if they are the same woman."

"She did," Jacob said. "For almost a month under both names. Bocci worked in the HR department of the corporation during the day, Hult worked graveyard as a shift assistant comp-troller, dealing with the money management at night."

"Wow," Halligan said. "That's some planning ahead. There is nothing in Hult's file from Brian that she was running from something or anyone. In fact, from Brian's file, her parents claimed she was happy, just bought a new home, a new car."

"Sandy Goodson had just bought a new home and a new car," Fawn said.

Halligan nodded and gave a thumbs up to Fawn. He knew that chances are that was just a coincidence, but in this case, everything felt important. It would be a tiny detail that would break it open.

"We'll check that with the rest of the victims," Jacob said. "But still not a clue as to why Hult did what she did and where she vanished to a second time in 2009."

"And who was helping her," Halligan said.

"Both Judy and I have been doing a deep dive into her life," Jacob said, "from the moment you told us what Brian said and we got Hult's picture from the casino. We want to know how she had the skills to set up that fake Bocci identity so that it held up so well under casino level investigations. Or who had the skills. Those were specialized skills in 1999. Impressive."

"What about the DNA from Sandy Goodson's sister? Any news on that yet?"

"Expecting it any moment," Jacob said. "I'll call you if we find anything in any of these searches."

"We'll be going through the files," Fawn said. "Looking for anything that doesn't fit."

"Good," Jacob said. "You need Young to help you?"

Halligan glanced at Fawn, who nodded.

"Hell, yeah," Halligan said and gave Jacob his address. "Send him over."

"Will do," Jacob said and hung up.

Halligan glanced at the boxes and the files they had already started to put out on the table. "Three sets of experienced eyes are better than two."

"Just hope you have enough coffee," Fawn said.

"Cabinets full of the stuff above the coffee maker," Halligan said. "Always deathly afraid I would run out of the stuff right when I needed it, so always bought extra."

"As if there aren't a dozen places within a mile of here to get coffee twenty-four seven," Fawn said, then laughed.

Halligan frowned. "Come on, a guy can have his fears."

Fawn again laughed, then said, "That one might take years of counseling to get over."

"Who says I want to get over it?" Halligan asked.

Fawn laughed and they both turned to the boxes of files in front of them.

CHAPTER NINETEEN

February 23rd, 2019
Henderson, Nevada

Young arrived at Halligan's place about thirty minutes after they started into the files. The three of them went to the kitchen to get Young a cup of coffee, then headed back to the files.

"Wow, you really don't live here much, do you?" Young said to Halligan, looking around at the unused and mostly empty rooms.

"Yeah," Halligan said. "Fawn's been helping me finally think about making the break."

Fawn liked the sound of that. A couple times she felt like she might have stepped over a line, but clearly Halligan was appreciating her help and that made her feel good. In just a few short days they had become partners and that felt great.

Young nodded. "I had the same decision, but finally decided to stay in my place because it's full of stuff, I actually use most of the house, and I love it and the location. You don't seem like you use much of this place?"

"And I don't much like it," Halligan said.

Young laughed. "And if admitting that doesn't get you off the dime, nothing will."

Halligan could only agree to that.

They started talking about how to organize what they had with all the files.

With the extra leaves for the table inserted, it was long enough that they could get eleven files side-by-side long ways. So Fawn cut up some paper and wrote each year from 1999 to 2009 on the pieces in big letters and taped them to eleven glasses and then put the glasses along one edge of the big table.

Sign posts through an ugly eleven years.

Then they took the March file from each year and put it under the glass. Then under March came the August file for each year.

Then the November file for each year.

When they finished getting all the files in chronological order, they stepped back and just stared.

Fawn could not believe how overwhelming it was seeing all thirty-three files covering the massive dining room table. And each file was a woman's life and a family that missed her.

"If this doesn't take your breath away, nothing will," Young said.

"What in the hell happened to all these women?" Halligan asked, softly.

"And that's what we are going to find out," Fawn said. And she planned on doing just that.

She picked up the Jean Hult file, the top one under 1999 and moved it to the bottom corner of the table, after the last file in 2009.

"We know what happened to her in 1999," Fawn said. "She became Angel Bocci and seems to be a part of all of this."

Both Halligan and Young nodded.

Fawn tapped Jean's file. "We find her, we find out what happened and why to all the rest of these women."

"Agreed," Halligan said. "Jacob and Judy are scouring every day of those years of Bocci's life. She had to have had a partner in all this. Phone records, receipts, anything should give us a clue as to how and where Bocci lived during those years."

"They will find something," Young said. "I've watched those two do miraculous things on those computers."

At that moment Fawn's phone chimed and she glanced at it and said, "Jabob" before clicking it on and saying, "Got all three of us."

"Got a close familial match on the DNA from Sandy Goodson's sister," Jacob said.

"You find Sandy?" Fawn asked, feeling her stomach twist.

"No," Jacob said. "But we found her sixteen-year-old son. Born in December, 2002. He was in the system because of an auto accident a year ago. He and his adopted family actually live in Summerlin."

"Son?" Young asked, shaking his head

"Born nine months after she vanished," Halligan said.

"Oh shit," Fawn said. And she meant it. She looked at all the folders on the table and then at the March, 2002, folder with Sandy Goodson's name on it.

"But we can find no evidence at all," Jacob said, "that she had a boyfriend at the time of her disappearance, or was even dating. In fact, we are pretty convinced from her social records that we can trace that Sandy Goodson was a lesbian. She had a very close companion by the name of Susan Down."

"Her sister did not know that," Halligan said.

That didn't surprise Fawn. Family often didn't know about gay family members, especially if there was a reason to not come out to the family.

"Reese said she and Sandy argued about Sandy dating," Halligan said. "Now we know why."

All three of them just stood there staring at all the files, shaking their heads. Fawn was having an impossible time trying to track the fact that Sandy Goodson had a son nine months after she was taken.

"In fact," Jacob said, "of most of the missing women that we are doing deep dives into their lives, they all seem to have very close girlfriends, not boyfriends. Judy and I are almost sure that most, if not all, were lesbians. And all still seemed to be deep in the closet when they vanished."

"Long before the time of same-sex marriage," Fawn said. Then she just felt tired and went over to a dining chair they had put in the corner of the room and just sat.

After a long few seconds, Jacob said, "Hello? Did we lose a connection?"

"No," Halligan said. "You just lost three jaded old cops trying to grasp what Sandy having a son means. We'll call you back shortly."

"I'm not old," Fawn said.

But honestly, at that very moment, she was feeling very old.

CHAPTER TWENTY

February 23rd, 2019
Henderson, Nevada

Halligan headed for the kitchen to not only get another cup of coffee, but to get away from the visual image of that massive table covered with thirty-three women's lives.

And he just needed to clear his head.

After a moment, as he poured himself another cup, Fawn and Young joined him.

He refreshed both of their cups, then dumped the rest of the pot out and proceeded to make a fresh pot. The mundane task of doing that was actually working to clear his head.

When he finished, he turned around. Young was sitting at the small glass kitchen table and Fawn was leaning against the wall.

"This is going to open up a lot of leads," Halligan said.

"Where was the baby born?" Fawn asked.

"Birth mother's fake name if the baby was born in a hospital," Young said.

"Was the baby adopted and by who and where did they get the baby?" Halligan asked.

"What did the adopting parents know?"

"Hang on," Young said. "We are jumping to the conclusion that Sandy Goodson didn't want to have a baby. Maybe there is some reason she did."

"After disappearing right out of thin air?" Fawn asked, shaking her head. "I'm betting that when Sandy Goodson started off to work that day, she had no intention of having a child nine months later."

Halligan laughed. "And we thought we had a mess before this?"

"So we need to find out if having a child is part of whatever was happening," Fawn said. "If there are more children out there."

"Let's contact Brian," Halligan said, "have him get swabs from a member of the family of the three women he searched for."

"Good idea," Fawn said.

"I think we need to contact the families of all the older cases," Halligan said. "More chances their DNA would have made it into the system somewhere."

"I can do that," Young said. "I'll set up in my office at home and with Judy's help find addresses for close family who is still alive and get that process started."

"And Brian can work on the three of his cases," Fawn said. "We might get lucky if there are more children out there. Or if the women are still alive somewhere."

Halligan nodded. "I like this. Fawn and I will dig into Sandy Goodson's son, see what rock we can uncover about his adoption."

"There is a chance that all this is about a baby mill," Young said.

"Damn, you had to go and say it aloud," Halligan said.

"One of us had to," Young said, smiling.

"Maybe it is," Fawn said. "But we need to figure out where all these women went, even if their abduction was for a baby mill."

Halligan agreed.

"Hang on," Fawn said and got Jacob on the phone.

"Can you look up if a baby mill was busted in this state or California around the time this ended?"

"Already did," Jacob said. "One was broken up here in 2011. It was kept pretty quiet because of the children and families involved. Didn't even make the paper."

"We need that case," Halligan said. "I honestly don't even remember a word about it.

"Andor will have it tomorrow for us," Jacob said. "Boxes of paperwork, one of the doctor's involved is still sitting in jail. The other two people who helped are dead. One suicide."

"Any sign that case was linked to what we are doing?" Fawn asked.

"No link at all yet," Jacob said.

"What happened to the women who had the children in that case?" Halligan asked.

"They were held on a farm about twenty miles up in the desert going east of town. Some of them had been forced to have six or seven babies. As the police closed in, the seven that were on the farm were killed and buried to try to hide what had been happening."

"Let's hope that isn't what this is," Fawn said.

Halligan could only agree with that. Especially with all the files on that table in the other room.

CHAPTER TWENTY-ONE

February 23rd, 2019
Henderson, Nevada

Fawn had been rocked by a lot of ugly things over all her years on the force, but the idea that all those women were taken for a baby farm hit her deep.

So now she had to get back to work and just focus, and she and Halligan were going to focus on the one kid they did know about, and trying to find out if Sandy Goodson was still alive, somehow, for some reason. She didn't believe that was possible, but now finding her son made everything possible.

Young had left to go home to start setting up searching for the families of the other missing women to get DNA swabs if he could.

Halligan from the kitchen called Brian and told him what they had found and got him started on contacting his three families to get DNA swabs from them. Fawn wandered back into the dining room with the files and called Jacob.

"Just me at the moment," Fawn said. "Young is headed back to his house to set up searches for the families of the older missing women."

"Better chance of having DNA in the system," Jacob said. "Judy will help him."

"Exactly. And Halligan is getting Brian doing the same thing. But then he and I are going to tackle the adoption of Sandy Goodson's son. Any information on any of that?"

"Adoption agency is a ghost," Jacob said. "All fake documents, licenses, names. It existed for one adoption and that was for the son of Sandy Goodson."

"So complete dead end," Fawn said, feeling angry at that. "And we can't trust anything from those records such as where he was born."

"Looks like it," Jacob said. "No records of his birth that we can find in any hospital. But the birth and adoption records are so well done, they would pass any kind of inspections except a deep dive like we are doing."

"Doctor of record?"

"Totally fake and that was the only case we can find that doctor listed anywhere."

"Damn it," Fawn said. "These people were good, very good, at covering all tracks."

"They were," Jacob said.

"So we need to focus on the adopting couple," Fawn said. "Are they rich?"

"No," Jacob said. "Just working-class level, which does not fit the pattern of a baby mill. And even more importantly, neither one of them existed before Sandy Goodson disappeared. Both their backgrounds are completely made up and done amazingly well. Especially for that time."

Fawn just stood there shaking her head. Without DNA, this

family would have been impossible to trace in any fashion. She glanced at all the other files on the big table. What in the world was going on?

"Even stranger," Jacob said. "The couple who adopted the boy is now divorced and the guy basically stopped existing after the divorce, if he ever existed at all. The woman remarried."

"Can you send us the current information on the family now, other kids, jobs, pictures, cars they own, banking, anything you can find?

"Putting all that together now," Jacob said. "Give us another half hour to make sure we didn't miss anything and we'll send it to you."

"Sounds great," Fawn said. "But text me their living address first and Halligan and I will get headed that way to do a drive-by."

"Will do," Jacob said.

"And one more thing," Fawn said as one loose end popped into her head. "Can you do a background check of the kid's DNA, see if you can find any reference to who the father might be?"

"Good idea," Jacob said. "Information on the way."

With that he hung up and Fawn headed back into the kitchen to get away from the sea of files for missing women.

Halligan was just standing in the kitchen, staring off into space, his coffee mug growing cold in his hands.

He noticed that she had come in, took a sip of his coffee, shook his head and dumped it out in the sink.

"Brian going for DNA?"

"He is," Halligan said.

"Talked to Jacob," Fawn said. "You are not going to believe what he found now."

And for the next few minutes in the kitchen she relayed what

Jacob had said, and then they headed out for Summerlin to see where Sandy Goodson's son lived. They both knew that there was nothing they could do there. But the drive would give them a chance to soak in everything they had learned and process it.

Just the idea that they might have uncovered a baby farm operation with over thirty women just felt impossible to digest. Actually, she didn't want to.

Fawn wasn't sure about Halligan, but there was no doubt she was in a light shock. And that was not conducive to clear thinking.

CHAPTER TWENTY-TWO

February 23rd, 2019
Henderson, Nevada

The driving helped clear Halligan's mind as he got them onto the freeway and headed at almost seventy past the Strip. It was just a little after two in the afternoon and the traffic was just moderate for a weekday afternoon.

Summerlin was directly across the entire Las Vegas valley from Henderson, a completely planned community designed and built by the Howard Hughes Corporation. Pre-planned subdivisions and malls and a carefully planned downtown area, all laid out in desert browns. It was a beautiful spread out on the side of the hill leading from downtown up into the red rocks, but not a place Halligan would ever want to live.

Plus even though his house in Henderson was worth over a million, it wouldn't touch the price tag of some of the mansions in Summerlin.

On the way Fawn had gotten the directions program

working on the car's dashboard and had plugged in the address of Sandy Goodson's son and adopted family. They had no intention of talking to anyone there. This entire drive was more of an excuse to give him and Fawn time to think about facing an entire baby factory ring.

Halligan always felt that the people who did that with children for money were far, far lower on the scale of scum than murderers. Thankfully, until now, he had never had to face anyone who had trafficked in babies.

"So what's the plan?" Fawn asked as they took the Summerlin Parkway branch of the freeway.

"Nothing," Halligan said. "Maybe just sit on the street and take some pictures if someone goes in and out."

"Our first stakeout together," she said. "We don't have the coffee, snacks, and sleeping masks to make this work."

"Sleeping masks?" he said, laughing.

"You don't think I stayed up all night on a stakeout, do you?" Fawn asked. "You're a barbarian and a girl's got to have her beauty sleep."

All Halligan could do was laugh. Finally he said, "I was thinking about an hour at most."

"Well, that's a relief," Fawn said, smiling at him.

And that exchange knocked him right out of the mindset of what they might be facing and back into figuring it all out.

"You getting the sense we are missing something in all this?" Halligan asked as he got off the freeway and followed the directions on the screen.

"Driving me crazy," Fawn said. "We got all these pieces and not a one of them make sense."

"Agreed," Halligan said. "For example, what changed in 2009 that they stopped?"

"Computers were a lot better and getting better quickly,"

Fawn said. "Maybe the people doing the hiding no longer felt they could keep it hidden?"

Halligan nodded, but that didn't feel right. "Maybe they had made enough money?"

Fawn shook her head. "Never heard of one of the types doing this ever thinking they had made enough money."

"Good point," Halligan said, turning off the main road and onto a winding subdivision road that went up hill. "Maybe they had enough women at that point."

"Address is the third house on the right," Fawn said, not answering his point, which he didn't blame her for. Not something he wanted to think about.

As they got near the house, Fawn pulled out her phone to get some pictures as they drove past.

The home was large and looked a lot like his mini-mansion in Henderson, except this was a brown stucco that matched the brown stucco of all the other houses along the street.

It was two-stories tall and had a three-car garage facing the street with a wide driveway. All the landscaping was desert plants done just exactly like all the other houses.

But Halligan could tell that on this side, out of the upstairs windows, there would be a fantastic view of the valley and the Strip in the distance and more than likely the view from the back was of the mountains. And he had no doubt there was a pool back there.

He went up the street a ways, then turned around and came back, parking across the street on the property line of two other homes and two houses up the street from where Sandy Goodson's kid lived.

He left the car running to keep the environmental controls inside on. Then they both just sat back to watch and rest a little bit.

Halligan had no expectations to see anything. And just sitting for the moment in silence with Fawn just felt right.

CHAPTER TWENTY-THREE

February 23rd, 2019
Summerlin, Nevada

Fawn really enjoyed sitting quietly with Halligan, staring down the suburban street at a large house that she doubted held any answers to the puzzle they were facing. But the sixteen-year-old boy who lived there by his very existence sure had opened up a ton more questions.

And Fawn really appreciated that Halligan was a type that didn't need to be talking all the time. The more time she spent with him, the more she was coming to really like him.

She had always liked him over all the years they had known each other, but she was coming to the conclusion that she hadn't really known him. And now she was getting to know him and she liked that a lot. More than she really wanted to admit at the moment.

After they had sat there for ten minutes, her phone rang. It was Jacob.

She put it through the car's speakers and said, "Hello. Got both Halligan and me sitting a couple houses up the street in front of Sandy Goodson's kid's home."

"Understood," Jacob said. "Got more information about the family that lives in that house and you won't believe it when I tell you."

Halligan looked at Fawn, shaking his head. "Now what?"

"The couple living there are Sandy and Susan Down," Jacob said.

"For hell's sake," Halligan said.

It took Fawn a moment, then she remembered that Susan Down had been Sandy Goodson's girlfriend when she disappeared. Both Halligan and Fawn had tried to find her when they first made a run at the case, but records showed that after Sandy disappeared, Susan had moved to the East Coast and pretty much vanished.

"Susan had a daughter a year after Sandy had her son," Jacob said. "They have been living first in Orange County in California, then after Sandy divorced her pretend husband, they moved back and got married as soon as Nevada law allowed them to."

"They have been a couple since before Sandy vanished?" Halligan asked.

"It seems that way," Jacob said.

"What about Susan's family?" Fawn asked. "Do they know?"

"They do not," Jacob said. "Only the father and one brother are left alive and as far as they know Susan moved to New York and then went missing there two months after Sandy vanished here. Susan's family filed a report there, but it went cold."

Fawn could feel an immense sense of relief flooding over her. They were not facing a baby mill after all.

"So you think this same thing happened to all those other women?" Halligan asked.

"We're not sure yet," Jacob said. "We're going to have to wait for more DNA and find the partners of the other women to really put the pattern together."

"And find out who helped them," Fawn said.

She glanced at Halligan and he nodded and smiled, clearly as relieved as she felt.

"Okay," Fawn said, "we're going to head back to Halligan's place and start searching through those files for any clue as to the partners."

"Young has managed to get three of the early families so far to allow a DNA test," Jacob said.

"We'll check in with Brian and tell him what you have found and see how he is doing," Fawn said.

"And Jacob," Halligan said, "remind Young and Judy and we'll remind Brian that we can't say anything about this to the families. Since it doesn't look like there is a crime, my gut sense is that none of these women want to be found by their family or by anyone from their old life."

"Understood," Jacob said and hung up.

"What an amazing relief," Fawn said. She so wanted to give Halligan a hug, but since they were both still strapped into the car, she just reached over and squeezed his arm.

And he just beamed back.

Then he said, "We still got a lot of pieces of this puzzle to put together. But my gut sense is that we are no longer looking for thirty-three dead women."

Fawn could only agree with that. And what a relief that was.

At that moment, a BMW SUV pulled into the driveway of the home they had been watching and parked. A slightly plump woman with short brown hair got out of the driver's side and on the other side a skinny blonde girl that looked to be about four-teen or fifteen or so got out.

Fawn quickly snapped pictures as the two walked into the house, laughing about something. It took Fawn a moment, but then she realized who she had been watching.

Different color hair, older, and forty pounds plumper, but that was Sandy Goodman.

Then when the front door closed, Fawn glanced at Halligan who was still staring at the house shaking his head and smiling.

"I've been haunted by Sandy Goodson's disappearance for seventeen years now," Halligan said, turning to face Fawn. "Never in a million years did I think I would see her get out of a car and walk into a home, laughing. I imagined a thousand other outcomes, but never once that."

All Fawn could do was smile. So many, many of her cases over the decades, just like Halligan's, had ended up with her staring at a body or the remains of a person.

Watching a live, happy person was very different.

Damn this felt good.

Better than good.

Wonderful!

CHAPTER TWENTY-FOUR

February 23rd, 2019
Summerlin, Nevada

Halligan started the car back down the street, smiling like a little kid who had just been given the Christmas present of their dreams. He had to admit that one of the reasons he had retired so early was because he felt he was getting jaded. He never looked to a positive outcome because so many hundreds of times there wasn't.

He wasn't sure that he had ever considered that Sandy had wanted to disappear when she had. He had always just assumed something bad had happened to her. So even seventeen years ago, the positive had already been knocked out of him.

"Damn," Fawn said, "if we didn't have so much more work to do to put the rest of the pieces of this puzzle together, I would suggest a large amount of drinking right about now."

"Oh, as soon as we get this all wrapped up, I'll take you up on that. And first round is on me, since I've been on this case the longest."

"Deal," Fawn said.

He liked the sound of that more than he wanted to admit.

"So are you a funny drunk, a sad drunk, an angry drunk?" Fawn asked.

"Been so long since I got drunk," Halligan said, "I don't remember. Cindy said I was a funny drunk. And an amorous one. How about you?"

"Funny and amorous as well, from what I have been told," Fawn said. "This could get real interesting."

He laughed and she laughed.

"Sadly," she said, "I can't remember the last time I had more than one drink."

"Me too," he said. "So let's figure out the missing pieces of this puzzle and where all the rest of those women ended up and make it a night to remember."

"Deal," she said. "What do we start on first?"

"DNA samples," Halligan said. "And then tracking girl-friend's names and see if they have been reported missing some-where and maybe get a few DNA samples from their families."

Fawn nodded. "More we got, the more chances of hits."

Then Halligan had an idea that might answer a few more questions. "How about we stop and talk with Reese, Sandy's sister?"

"Why in the world would we want to do that?" Fawn asked. "We can't tell her a thing about what we have found?"

"I know," Halligan said. "We can be looking for more back-ground is all. I would love to know what Sandy's family life was like around the topic of being gay?"

"To find out why Sandy would do such a drastic action like she did?" Fawn asked, nodding. "I'd like to know that as well."

"And we can be very careful. As far as Reese is concerned, we're just trying to find any leads at all."

"I'll call her," Fawn said, taking out her phone.

Halligan nodded. They would both have to be very careful, but they could do that.

Twenty minutes later Halligan had them parked in front of Sandy's sister's home and Reese met them on the front porch. The afternoon was warm, but not too warm and it felt good to Halligan to be outside.

"Kids doing homework," she said as she pulled the door closed behind her.

"No problem," Fawn said. "We won't be long and thanks for seeing us."

"Any progress?" Reese asked.

"Afraid not," Halligan lied. "That's why we wanted to talk with you just a little more, see if we could get a handle on something. Anything."

"So," Fawn said, her notebook in her hand, "you said that Sandy didn't have anyone she was dating. Any boyfriend at all?"

"Not a one," Reese said.

"How about girlfriends?" Halligan asked. "Anyone Sandy might have confided with?"

"I wouldn't know about that," Reese said.

Halligan noticed that was just a little bit charged.

"Was Sandy having female friends a problem?" Fawn asked.

"Our parents were very religious," Reese said. "Our entire family, actually. Before our parents were killed, my mother caught Sandy making out with another girl. She put Sandy in a program to try to help her get past those tendencies."

Reese almost spit out the word tendencies.

Halligan nodded, but managed to keep a poker face so Reese couldn't tell how disgusted he felt.

Fawn nodded, staying blank as well and changed the topic. "How about Sandy's job? Did she like it?"

"She seemed to," Reese said. "It allowed her to buy that house and her car. She seemed happy and as the job went on, she got more and more so."

Halligan again nodded. That made sense as well. Clearly the job was the way that Sandy found Angel Bocci and the ability to be with the woman she loved.

"Again, please don't get your hopes up," Halligan said. "Seventeen years is a very long time."

"But we are doing what we can," Fawn said. "We'll keep you informed. Thanks for your time."

"Thank you, detectives," Reese said.

With that they headed back to the car and all Halligan wanted to do was get them away from there and the disgust he felt for Reese. Motive is always an important factor in any case and they had just established clearly why Sandy wanted to just disappear, start over.

"All I want to do is take a shower after that?" Fawn said.

"How about lunch instead?"

"Perfect," Fawn said. "You like Mexican food?"

Halligan laughed and then said, "Seriously, you just asked a Las Vegas detective if he liked Mexican food?"

Fawn laughed. "Sorry, wasn't thinking."

CHAPTER TWENTY-FIVE

February 23rd, 2019
Henderson, Nevada

Fawn couldn't remember a lunch she had enjoyed so much. In fact she doubted there were two detectives in the entire city in as good a mood as they were. And why not? Their case had just gone from trying to find out what happened to thirty-three women and where their bodies were buried and who had forced them to have babies for sale to the chance all the women were alive and happy with their partners.

Fawn was pretty sure that the people in the booth next to them had left early because she and Halligan were making too much noise. And Fawn flat didn't care.

When they got back to Halligan's place, the files covering the massive table seemed completely different. Instead of over-whelming gloom, they seemed to almost glow. Amazing what an attitude change could make.

Halligan went into the kitchen and came back a minute later

with two mugs of coffee and a big black felt-tip pen. He took Sandy's file from its position on the table and wrote "Solved" in big letters on the front, then smiled and dropped it into one of the banker's boxes.

"Can't begin to say how good that felt."

"Agree," Fawn said. Then she stared at the expanse of files in front of her. "I hope like hell we can do that with a lot of the others as well."

Halligan nodded.

"The woman I still want to talk with is Angel or Jean or whoever she might be now," Fawn said, tapping Jean's file. "There had to be some money and an organization behind all this. I hope Brian can get a DNA sample from her family. I think she is the key to writing solved on all of these."

"Let's find out how Brian's doing and get him updated."

Brian answered the phone quickly and Fawn put her phone on speaker. Then for the next ten minutes they told him what they had found.

All Brian could do was just laugh.

"You know," Brian said after they finished the recap, "I've been thinking of retiring and this just might be the note to go out on."

"Can't tell anyone why, of course," Halligan said, "but if you're throwing a retirement party, I'll sure be there."

"You both are invited," Brian said.

"We're still hoping you got DNA from the families."

"Picked all three up earlier this morning and dropped them at Young's house. I had expected the DNA might lead us to some bodies."

"This is a whole lot better," Halligan said.

"Can only agree to that," Brian said. "Just too bad the families will never know what happened."

"Well, might not be too bad," Fawn said. Then she told him about what Sandy's sister had said and her attitude.

"Real good point," Brian said. "Two of these families I've dealt with are real radical religious. Pieces are falling together now."

"All these women clearly had a reason to vanish from an old life to live a new life," Halligan said. "And thank heavens vanishing is not a crime."

"My sense is that these women were running from abuse, intolerance, violence, maybe even death threats," Fawn said. "All we could do would be to bring that ugliness back into their lives and I for one don't want to do that."

"Totally agree," Brian said.

Halligan was nodding.

"We'll keep you posted on what we find as we try to put more of this crazy puzzle together," Fawn said.

"Thanks," Brian said. "You can't begin to know how much this has made my day, my week, hell, even the year."

Fawn and Halligan both laughed, then Halligan said, "Our service isn't cheap, but we aim to please."

Brian laughed and said, "We're not going there."

And he cut the connection.

"I think we might be a little punchy," Fawn said, laughing as she put her phone away.

"You think?" Halligan asked, and smiled that wonderful smile Fawn could get real used to.

CHAPTER TWENTY-SIX

February 23rd, 2019
Henderson, Nevada

Two hours and three cups of coffee later, Halligan put the last file back in place and stood and stretched. They had a list of twenty girlfriends from the files and they might as well get it to Jacob so he could do his magic computer work. More than likely Jacob had already got most of the names anyway. But it didn't hurt to double-check everything.

Fawn called Jacob and put him on speaker and told him that they had found twenty girlfriends in the files.

"Twenty?" Jacob said. "That's four more than we found. Hang on."

Halligan just grinned at Fawn. Seems that sometimes old-fashioned police work beat computers.

"Go through the names and which file they belong to," Jacob said.

Fawn and Jacob spent the next ten minutes making sure all the names matched. Actually Jacob had missed five and they had missed one.

"You can also close the Melissa Singles file," Jacob said. "She was one of the early, first-year ones and we discovered she died of cancer two years ago in Colorado."

"Kids?" Fawn asked."

"Nope just her marriage partner."

Jacob gave them the date of death and Halligan wrote solved on the file and deceased and put that file in the box. Not the way he wanted to close these files, but at least she got to live the life she wanted for a decade or more.

"Any movement on Angel Bocci/Jean Hult?" Halligan asked.

"DNA will be back tomorrow on about eight of them, including her family," Jacob said. "Got a friend in a lab in California going to stay up all night getting us preliminary results."

Both Fawn and Halligan were shaking their heads at that. Normal time through the force would be months. This was damn near the speeds of fake cop shows on television. Almost.

"Well, that will give us a shot at finding a few more," Halligan said, looking at the table.

"Maybe establish a pattern we can trust," Fawn said.

"The girlfriends will help as well," Jacob said.

"What will really help is we find Jean Hult," Halligan said.

"Agreed," Jacob said. "I'll call you if there is any more progress."

Fawn put her phone away and stood beside Halligan staring at the table of missing person's files.

The silence filled the room for a minute, then Halligan said, "I want to clear every one of these. How do we do that after clearing four or five with finding the spouses, maybe a couple with DNA? That's still going to leave over twenty missing person's cases."

"I agree," Fawn said. "No drinking until this table is clear."

Halligan laughed and glanced at Fawn, who was smiling slightly. "Now that might be a little extreme, don't you think?"

"Maybe a touch," Fawn said.

Then Halligan laughed. "You know, I wonder if anyone has told Andor and the Chief of our progress today?"

"Oops," Fawn said, also laughing.

She got out her phone and got Andor on speaker and spent the next half hour giving him all the good news. And what they were still working on.

"Oh, my god," Andor said after they were finished. "The Chief is going to be ecstatic and bummed at the same time. Happy about closing some of these tough cases, bummed he can't tell the press."

"Ahh, I'm sad for the Chief," Fawn said.

Andor just laughed.

"And tell Detective Little he got lucky," Halligan said. "The paperwork on all this is going to be minor, if any. Better than a graveyard full of bodies."

"Might get to see the big guy dance a happy dance," Andor said.

"Film it," Fawn said.

"Damn straight," Andor said, laughing. And then hung up.

At that Halligan glanced back at the table still full of files. "You think we might be done for the night?"

"I think we just might be," Fawn said.

"Steak dinner on me," Halligan said. "To celebrate how this turned good instead of ugly."

"Drinking when we clear the table," Fawn said, nodding. "Steak it is."

Halligan led the way to his car and to one of the best and most enjoyable dinners he could remember in a very, very long time.

CHAPTER TWENTY-SEVEN

February 24th, 2019
Henderson, Nevada

Fawn woke up the next morning early to go on her run and halfway through the 5K normal run around her suburban neighborhood streets, one word sprang into her head. "Money."

The morning was cool, but the sun was out so it felt fine. And no wind. Sometimes the wind this time of the year was much worse than the cold. Running in hard wind was just no fun.

But this morning it was great. Cool and calm, with sun. Perfect. All of which helped her already great mood from the wonderful steak dinner last night with Halligan. They had gone to a place on Flamingo about three blocks off the Strip where Fawn swore the steaks had been soaked in butter before they grilled them.

Melt in your mouth tender. And they had both overdone the

quantity of butter rolls. She lost count after six. And even though she was stuffed when she got home, she slept like a rock.

After just two days, she was really enjoying being with Halligan. More than she ever would have imagined. And a couple times last night she had caught herself just staring at him like a dumb teenager.

And she caught him once just staring at her, so she had a hunch the increased feelings were mutual.

So as she turned the corner in front of the main gate of Palm Water Subdivision, the word "money" sprang into her mind, and that turned all her thinking away from Halligan to the case.

These women all disappeared from Las Vegas, all leaving everything behind, including money. Now that it was seeming likely they had all lived, how did they survive?

Someone had been there, more than likely a group with some pretty deep pockets.

That meant that the women almost immediately had to set up a checking account somewhere, more than likely within days of vanishing, with seed money from somewhere. And since she and Halligan knew where Sandy was, Fawn bet that Jacob and Judy could trace Sandy's bank accounts back to when she vanished.

And if they could figure out how Sandy had been helped, Fawn bet money that they could find a pattern in all the cases. And that might just be the way to solve every remaining case on the table.

That is if all the cases were as clear-cut as Sandy's had been. As a long-term detective, Fawn still had her doubts about so much of this. She was just too used to living in the underside of the criminal world to believe in too many happy endings.

And then as Fawn was getting close to seeing her condo and

the end of her normal morning run, another thought hit her. They had assumed that someone had helped them just to help them escape. But what happens if Sandy and the others had to pay a price for that help?

"Damn it all to hell," she said to herself as she picked up speed through the last half block before getting to the complex. "Just damn it."

Because making the women pay some sort of price made a ton more sense than just a nice person giving them money because they were gay.

What was the price?

Suddenly the wonderful, clear, crisp morning just didn't feel so wonderful.

CHAPTER TWENTY-EIGHT

February 24th, 2019
Henderson, Nevada

Halligan had just loved the dinner the night before. It wasn't often that two detectives got to celebrate good news. And even more so, he was really starting to like Fawn. More than just as a partner, but he flat didn't yet want to think about that.

It wasn't until he walked by the dining room in his house, getting a cup of coffee before going to picking up Fawn that something hit him. That was a lot of women who had started over.

He stood there staring at the huge table covered in files, his hot mug of coffee in his hands, too hot to drink.

If all of the women were still alive, as they were starting to assume because of Sandy's case, how in the world had they afforded to live before getting new identification and getting a job? Every one of them had left a car, most if not all had homes they left, none had taken money out of their accounts ahead of time.

It took money to live and, as Sandy did, travel to California and start over there.

Money was the key to solving all these case. But even worse, what did all those women have to do in exchange for that money?

How much did they pay?

And at what price?

Halligan took his coffee to his car and ten minutes later was sipping on it in front of Fawn's condo complex. The place was five stories tall, light tan stucco, and formed a U-shape. A five-story parking garage took up the back side, making the entire thing a big square and Fawn said there was a lovely pool in the middle.

She said every condo had either a great view over the valley or a view over the pool.

Halligan actually liked the idea of a big pool more than the views. He used to be a swimmer and wouldn't mind getting back to it to stay fit.

Fawn came out carrying a cup of coffee as well and seemed in a bright mood, just as he had been before thinking about the money.

But just seeing her made him smile.

She was coming down the sidewalk headed directly for his car. She had on jeans, a white blouse covered by a suit-like light blue jacket. Her red hair seemed to shine even brighter in the sun, and even though just over five-foot tall, she strode like she was six-foot and in control of everything.

She had her sunglasses tucked above her forehead into her hair and she smiled a huge smile when she saw him.

All he could think of was "Damn she is good-looking."

More than likely he was smiling, which kept him from just staring like a fool with his mouth open.

He had on his standard jeans and running shoes, but today had put on one of his nicest dress shirts and a newer form-fitting sports coat.

"Morning," she said, climbing in beside him, putting her coffee into the holder beside his and patting his arm before putting on her seat belt. "Nice coat."

"Thanks," he said, happy she had noticed. "That was a really fun dinner."

She smiled even brighter, if that was possible, and again touched his arm. "It really was and I am still stuffed."

"Not too stuffed for breakfast?" he asked.

"Oh, never," she said, laughing. "You'll learn that the reason I run every morning is so that I can eat as much as I want anytime I want. And trust me, I can eat."

As he backed them out and headed for the same restaurant they had had breakfast at yesterday, he asked, "I thought you loved the running?"

"Oh, I do," she said. "But on nasty days I use the food to keep me going."

It didn't take him long to get to the restaurant and they ended up back in the exact same booth as yesterday.

"Morning, detectives," the owner said as he filled their coffee cups and sat the pot down. "Big case, huh?"

"Every day," Fawn said and smiled at him.

The owner laughed and said, "Crime never rests." Then he headed for the kitchen area.

"Speaking of crime," Fawn said. "Had some thoughts about how we find the other thirty women."

"Money," Halligan said.

She laughed. "Exactly. But afraid there is more than that?"

"Yeah, me too," Halligan said. "What did they have to do to get the help and the money?"

"How we think alike scares me sometimes," Fawn said, shaking her head.

"Honestly I kind of like it," Halligan said.

She laughed and picked up her coffee cup. "I will toast to that."

"So how about we check in with Jacob," Halligan said, "and see if he is working the same lines."

"After we order," Fawn said, indicating the waitress was heading their way.

This morning they both ordered ham and cheese omelets with toast and orange juice. Actually Fawn had ordered first and it sounded so good, he just doubled it.

Since there was no one near the booth, when Jacob answered Fawn put him on speaker, but on a low enough volume that Halligan and Fawn both had to lean in to hear.

"So we were wondering about where these women got the money to start over," Fawn said. "You started down that path yet?"

"Just getting to it," Jacob said.

"Thinking that since everything was so exactly done the same," Halligan said, "the pattern for Sandy might help you find the pattern for the rest of them, right down to how much was deposited and how each account was opened and when in relationship to the date of disappearance."

"Oh, really good thinking," Jacob said. "We can set that search up easily. But the lead we were starting to trace that might work just as well is that Sandy is still getting money in her account every month. Actually so is her partner Susan."

"How much?" Fawn asked.

"They are basically getting paid $6,500 each per month,"

Jacob said. "It's a salary, handled like they are both employees, with taxes and everything taken out."

"How soon after Sandy officially vanished did this start?" Fawn asked, looking as stunned as Halligan felt.

"Within a month," Jacob said. "It was a much smaller amount then, since it seems they have both gotten raises along the way."

"A month?" Fawn asked.

"A month," Jacob repeated. "And it seems that the fake names and identification had been created before Sandy vanished. So she had completely planned to vanish that day. In fact, we figure that she drove the car to the drop spot and walked away to be picked up in a camera-free area."

"What's the name of the company paying them?" Halligan asked.

"ASR Inc."

"You're kidding me," Fawn said, sitting back in the booth.

Halligan had never heard of the company, but clearly Fawn had.

"What do they do?" Halligan asked.

"They are a world-wide conglomerate," Jacob said, "specializing in everything from publishing self-help books to holding seminars for self-improvement and relationships. ASR supposedly stands for A Stable Relationship, but no one knows for certain. Some people think it stands for the names of the founders' original three cats, Abbot, Sammy, and Raines."

"Who were the founders?" Fawn asked.

"Two very recluse women," Jacob said. "Both died fantastically wealthy in the late seventies, leaving the company to their three children, all girls, who have continued to grow the business to multinational levels."

"Can you tell what Sandy is doing for the company?" Fawn asked.

"No," Jacob said. "And we are not finding much of a way to see if the other missing women work for them or not because of name changes and fantastically tight corporate security. The DNA is due to be back here in the next hour. I'll call you if we find more."

"Thanks," Fawn said and hung up just as breakfast arrived.

Halligan couldn't even begin to wrap his head around what he had just heard, so instead he focused on the omelet and the coffee.

Mostly the coffee.

CHAPTER TWENTY-NINE

February 24th, 2019
Henderson, Nevada

Fawn worked at her omelet for a few minutes while they both ate in silence, the sounds of the restaurant banging around them like a blanket covering them. She wasn't really tasting her food at all, except for the strong coffee. Somehow that taste seemed to get through.

She couldn't grasp that Sandy had been paid almost from moment one by a major corporation. Why and for what?

Not a bit of this was making any kind of sense. And Fawn still couldn't get her mind away from feeling that something was wrong here. Major corporations did all kinds of charity work, but not to the tune of over six thousand a month for years.

And if Sandy was getting paid like an employee, it would stand to reason that she must be doing something for the corporation. But what?

Fawn was just confused.

"Okay," Halligan said after a few minutes. "Let me ask a few questions that need to be answered here before my poor brain can start to make sense of this."

"Fire away," Fawn said, pulling out her notebook to write down anything they might come up with.

"We got over thirty files on that table," Halligan said. "All with the same exact circumstances of vanishing, all timed exactly."

Fawn nodded, letting him go on.

"I understand why Sandy wanted to get away, vanish, from that sister to be with the woman she loved," Halligan said. "And I am sure there were other women in the exact same position."

Again Fawn just nodded.

"But over thirty women willing to give up everything like that, their families, their lives, all like clockwork every so many months, three different women a year. Now *that* I have trouble wrapping my mind around."

Fawn hadn't thought of it that way. It did seem very unusual when put that way. So she wrote that down, having no answer at all for Halligan.

"Not all the women were from Las Vegas," Halligan said. "But they had all lived here for a year or more and all vanished from here."

"Maybe," Fawn said, "they moved here to get in line for vanishing and to get away from family and others who judged them for being gay."

Halligan nodded. "Nothing would surprise me about this. But we can't assume they were all gay or wanted to vanish for the same reasons. Once we find some of the others, we can trace their partners as well. Set up some patterns."

At that moment Fawn's phone buzzed. It was Jacob so once

again she put it on speaker, but low enough to not be heard by anyone but the two of them.

"DNA came back," Jacob said before she could even say hello. "We got matches. More children for the most part except for a few family members."

"Anything linking to Bocci/Hult?" Halligan asked an instant before Fawn did.

"Yes," Jacob said. "We got a link to her daughter. Jean Hult is her name still and she is living here in town in the Henderson area. In fact, she's a neighbor of yours, Halligan. Just a couple houses away."

Halligan sat back shaking his head.

"How many did you find?" Fawn said.

"We were able to trace the address of five of the missing women," Jacob said. "We're doing deep computer searches now, but it looks like they all had kids, three of them live here in the region, two over in southern California."

"Wow," Fawn said.

"Does the pattern of Sandy still hold?" Halligan asked.

"From as far as we can tell, it does," Jacob said. "All are married, and we think but haven't confirmed completely yet that all are being paid by ASR as employees, including Jean Hult."

"Are all gay?" Fawn asked.

"These five are and all married now to their partners."

"Any luck getting into ASR's records?" Halligan asked.

"Nothing," Jacob said. "For an organization focused on teaching and self-help, for some reason they have computer security levels above most governments. And only so much we dare try without warrants."

"And disappearing isn't a crime, so none of those coming," Fawn said.

"Exactly," Jacob said. "We'll keep digging for a little bit

longer, then send you the names and information of the ones we found so you can close those cases."

"Thanks," Fawn said. "Great work."

"Thanks," Jacob said and clicked off.

"So what do we do now?" Fawn asked, putting her phone back in her pocket.

"Drink coffee," Halligan said.

She laughed. "Is that your solution to most things?"

"Actually," he said, smiling over the rim of his cup, "it is. And it feels like the only solution to most of this, to be honest."

All Fawn could do was nod to that.

CHAPTER THIRTY

February 24th, 2019
Henderson, Nevada

Halligan got them headed back to his house. They were riding in silence, which Halligan realized about halfway there that he wasn't bothered by. He was so comfortable with Fawn, they didn't need to talk. On a couple of his partners over the years, he had never gotten to that point.

Finally Fawn turned to him. "I'm stuck on the employee status. This is a major corporation, international corporation. Audits and payroll issues would come up with any kind of charity aspects."

"Agreed," Halligan said, but said nothing more, waiting for her to finish.

"So Sandy and her partner are both actually doing something for the corporation."

Halligan shrugged. "Maybe all this was nothing more than a giant recruiting program."

Fawn shook her head. "At this point, that makes more sense than anything."

"I'm just glad we're not out looking for where there are thirty-three women's bodies," Halligan said.

"Or where they are being held and forced to have children that are sold," Fawn said.

"Yeah, that too."

They rode in silence to the gate to his subdivision and as it opened, Fawn said, "I think part of the problem here is that we are not used to investigating cases that might have happy endings."

"Cases like that seldom were something us detectives were handed," Halligan said, laughing. "But I think you are right. I just don't know how to think on this kind of thing where there is no body buried in the desert or a criminal taking money."

As he pulled into his driveway, Fawn agreed to that and a few minutes later he was marking solved on five of the folders, still leaving the table mostly covered.

Halligan wrote solved in big black marker on Jean Hult's file and handed it to Fawn. "I still think she can help us with the rest of these."

Fawn nodded. "And maybe answer a few of the questions about why?"

With that Fawn took out her phone and dialed a number and as Jacob came on the line, she said, "Got us both. I'm wondering if you have discovered what Jean Hult does for ARS?"

"We still are having no luck finding any kind of way into their records," Jacob said, "that doesn't break about a billion laws. But we did discover in a few of the business sites that are public facing that she is a vice president and came up out of HR."

"Well, shit," Halligan said. "I might not be wrong about this all being a recruiting drive."

"You might not be," Jacob said. "Of the five women we found, we were able to get bank account information and all of them are being paid as employees by ARS."

"All of them?" Fawn asked.

"Yes," Jacob said. "And we find no records at all that any of them were ever in touch with their families since they vanished."

"Thank you," Fawn said. "Can you get the phone number of Jean Hult?"

"Hang on," Jacob said.

Halligan just watched as Fawn wrote the number down and then thanked Jacob and hung up.

"You thinking we need to just go talk with her?" Halligan said.

"I do, if Andor and the Chief say it is all right."

Halligan nodded. "You call them, I'll make the coffee. Good luck."

"Chicken," Fawn said, laughing.

"Hey," he said, smiling back. "Making coffee is hard work."

CHAPTER THIRTY-ONE

February 24th, 2019
Henderson, Nevada

Fawn was still on the phone with Andor, on hold while Andor talked with the Chief, when Halligan came back with a mug of coffee for her. It was hot and tasted wonderful.

When Andor came back, Fawn said, "Got us both on the line."

"The answer is yes," Andor said. "As long as you are damned careful and make sure you are clear that as far as we can tell, no laws were broken and no one is in trouble and no one will report what we have found in any way."

"Exactly," Fawn said.

"The Chief wants us to pull the plug on this one," Andor said. "So this is pretty much the last shot at getting information."

"Understood," Halligan said.

"Yeah, it will be nice to get back to brutal murders and headless corpses," Fawn said, shaking her head.

"That's why we all get the big bucks," Andor said.

"I'm still trying to find this big buck thing everyone talks about," Halligan said.

"Yeah, me too," Andor said. "Be damned careful."

With that, he clicked off.

"So we got the green light," Fawn said. "Now what?"

Halligan pointed to the number she had written down. "Call her, set up an appointment."

Fawn nodded. She knew she needed to be the one to do it. So she took a deep breath and dialed the number and put it on speaker so Halligan could hear, but indicated he should remain silent and he nodded.

He quickly took out his notebook in case he needed to write her a note. And to take notes of what was said as well.

A secretary or receptionist answered the phone with "Jean Hult's office."

"This is retired Detective Isadora Fawn of the Metro Police Department. I would like to speak with Jean Hult on a private matter if that would be possible."

Fawn knew that she had needed to add the retired aspect in, but more than likely only the police stuff would be noted.

"Please hold," the receptionist said.

A moment later a deep woman's voice came back, "This is Jean Hult. How may I help you?"

"I am retired Detective Isadora Fawn. My partner and I are working a case for a special task force called The Cold Poker Gang task force. We have been investigating some missing person's cold case files and would like to talk to you. We understand that no crime has been committed and that nothing can be disclosed."

"If I talk with you," Jean said, "would you call off your computer people digging into our records and lives?"

Fawn glanced at Halligan who was trying not to cough and laugh at the same time.

"We are about to shut this investigation down," Fawn said. "So yes, I can do that as soon as I hang up with you."

"Thank you," Jean said. "I assume you are at retired Detective Hugh Halligan's house, which is three doors up the street from my home, I can meet you there in thirty minutes."

"That would be perfect," Fawn said. "And thank you for your time."

"See you shortly," Jean said and hung up.

"Holy shit," Halligan said. "When Jacob said they were good, he meant it."

Fawn was feeling shocked, that same feeling that she felt in a case when something had just turned upside down. "We have been watched the entire time. How was that even possible without us seeing it?"

"A seventeen-year-old missing person's case," Halligan said. "Not something that would have us watching for high-level surveillance."

Fawn nodded and quickly dialed Jacob.

After she explained what she had agreed to and what she had said and what the Chief had wanted, Jacob said, "Wow, they caught us. Sorry detectives. That will never happen again."

"Caught all of us," Halligan said.

"We'll shut down completely and scrub our computers, see if we can figure out what went wrong and why."

With that Jacob clicked off.

"Got a hunch the kids just learned some major lessons from this one," Halligan said. "There really are computer and security people out there better than they are."

"But maybe not for long," Fawn said. "Our team might have just gotten stronger because of this."

"Certainly more cautious no matter the type of case," Halligan said.

Fawn could only nod and agree to that.

CHAPTER THIRTY-TWO

February 24th, 2019
Henderson, Nevada

Halligan debated with the idea of cleaning off the table, then just figured that more than likely Jean had already seen pictures of the table since her security people were so good, so instead while they waited, they went into the kitchen and Halligan made a fresh pot of coffee. He had to admit, the rich smell was wonderful and calmed his nerves some.

He had no idea why he was nervous. He had faced some pretty hardened serial killers in his days. All this woman did was decide to go missing over twenty years ago. And then had clearly helped a lot of other women do the same thing.

Halligan suddenly realized he was nervous because he was impressed with what this woman had done. And that he had so many unanswered questions he hoped she would answer.

The doorbell rang right on time and Fawn said, "Here we go."

She was clearly nervous as well.

They both had their badges on and guns in their underarm holsters when Fawn answered the door, not because they feared the woman but to make sure she really understood who they were.

The woman standing on the porch was someone Halligan recognized from seeing her drive by, often in the mornings as he was leaving for work. And he recognized her from her twenty-year-old missing person's picture in her folder on the dining room table.

This woman was as short as Fawn, maybe shorter, and had thickened up some, but still looked to be in shape. Her dark hair was pulled back off her face and she wore a tan business suit. She didn't carry a purse and her low-heeled shoes looked like they were comfortable to walk in.

"Jean Hult?" Fawn asked. "I'm retired detective Fawn and this is retired detective Halligan. It's a pleasure to meet you."

Jean smiled and the smile actually reached her eyes. "Better than finding my skeleton in a mass grave as you expected, I bet."

Halligan and Fawn both laughed.

"I can't begin to tell you how much better," Halligan said as he and Fawn both stepped back to allow Jean to enter.

"Nice place," Jean said, glancing around.

"Empty," Halligan said. "I'm going to be moving shortly as soon as I figure out where. Kitchen is the most comfortable place to talk."

They headed that way with Jean only giving a glance at the dining room table as they went past. As Halligan had expected, she had seen it or seen pictures of it."

After Jean agreed to a cup of coffee, Fawn said, "We have our computer people shutting down, if they have not already done so."

"They are amazingly good," Jean said. "It was everything my people could do to stay ahead of them. In fact, your people are the only ones who even got close and gave us a scare. They are that good."

Halligan again laughed. "Nice of you to say, but fairly certain we won't tell them that. The fact that your people did stay ahead of them is going to eat at them for a very long time."

"And I bet that's a good thing," Jean said, smiling.

"Might save lives down the road," Fawn said. "Considering the line of work we are in normally."

Jean nodded, took a sip of the coffee, then set the cup down and said, "You realize that not a one of the women we have helped wants to be found by their family."

"We will not even put this conversation or any details in any of the files," Fawn said. "From what we have discovered, the women were getting away from abusive situations in some cases and we have no intention of breaking the law by revealing their locations."

"In all cases that's what they were escaping," Jean said. "That's one reason we have such great computer people working for us. Why it is an entire department. They monitor and protect the women we have helped. And so many others besides."

Halligan nodded. "That makes sense. Do all the women you have helped work for ARS?"

Jean shrugged. "Some do, yes. Others have moved on, gone to school, gotten new jobs. But they all did to start."

"Are there more than the 33 cases we found?" Fawn asked.

"Yes, many more," Jean said. "And that's all I can say about that."

Halligan sat back, not really shocked. Once they started to realize what was happening, there was no reason it would be limited to the 33 cases they found.

"Can I ask," Fawn said, leaning forward, "that if one of our cold case task force starts into an investigation of a missing woman that is one of yours and your computer people spot the investigation, could you let us know nothing more than that she is all right?"

"So you can move on to others who really need the help?" Jean asked. Then nodded. "We can do that. I will set that as a future policy."

"Thank you," Fawn said.

Halligan was getting a very good feeling about this Jean. But he still had so many questions.

"May I ask how you managed to be so regular on your disappearance schedule?" Halligan asked.

"We had so many who needed the help," Jean said, "we didn't dare go any faster, so sadly some had to wait up to two years for us to get them out of their situations."

"All gay women?" Fawn asked.

"In the program you uncovered and that I ran for a decade, yes," Jean said. "In other programs it has turned out to be about one gay man, or transsexual, out of every ten. Often the men are very young. Experienced gay men don't turn to programs like ours for help getting away from family and bad situations, even though we offer."

All Halligan could do was nod at that.

CHAPTER THIRTY-THREE

February 24th, 2019
Henderson, Nevada

After almost an hour of questions, Fawn had a very good detective sense of Jean. She didn't always give a full answer, but she said when she could not.

And the mood around the kitchen table had changed dramatically over the hour, from one of tension to one of trust.

It seemed that Jean respected Fawn and Halligan as equals in fighting to do the right thing. Jean just had the massive resources of a major corporation behind her. Granted, helping people vanish wasn't always a good solution, but Fawn over the years had helped numbers of people vanish into witness protection. There wasn't a great deal of difference when it was boiled down.

Sometimes vanishing for a person was just the correct option.

And the fact that the corporation that funded all this also

kept a very close and protective eye on those they helped sure was a benefit.

"One last question from me," Halligan said. "Why cut it at 2009? Was that because the laws started to ease up?"

"Attitudes were freeing up in some places," Jean said, nodding. "But the Supreme Court legalizing marriage equality nationwide wasn't until 2015. No we stopped because I got promoted and had trained a different person to find those who needed our help. So we didn't stop, just that one program ceased. Nothing has really changed when it comes to the bigotry faced by so many within their own friends and family circles."

Halligan nodded.

"I also only have one more question," Fawn said. "Why did ARS get started doing this?"

Jean smiled and pushed her coffee cup aside. "It is no secret that the two founders were a couple. So right from the start they helped other gay and lesbian couples because they had the money and resources to do so. And two of their daughters are also openly lesbian who now run the company."

Fawn started to say something, but Jean held up her hand.

"But the honest reason is recruiting," Jean said. "Half of our computer department that stayed ahead of your people were recruited in this fashion. And helping a person at this level builds in a natural level of loyalty, as you might imagine."

Fawn and Halligan both nodded.

"In fact," Jean said, "to answer that question fully, Fawn could you meet me tomorrow at Mandalay Bay Convention Center, at the Starbucks in the main hallway? About 8 am?"

"No problem," Fawn said.

"Sorry, Detective Halligan," Jean said, smiling. "You would not fit in."

Halligan nodded.

"Until tomorrow morning, then," Jean said, standing. "And thank you both for being so professional."

"It was a pleasure," Halligan said. "And as a jaded old detective, it feels great to have other good guys doing good work."

"At 55," Jean said, smiling, "you are not old."

"That's what I've been saying," Fawn said.

Halligan laughed. "Okay, replace old with retired."

"From what I see with the work the Cold Poker Gang task force does," Jean said, "you are all a long way from retiring."

"She has a point," Fawn said, laughing. "And this was just our first case."

At that moment they had reached the dining area and Jean went in to look at the case files on the table.

Fawn glanced at Halligan and he just shrugged, so they both stood quietly.

After scanning the entire table but not touching a file, Jean said, "I can tell you that all of these women are alive and safe except for this one."

She picked up a file and sighed. "She was a close friend. She died in a car wreck in another state just over a year ago."

Jean handed the file to Fawn, then said, "See you in the morning, detective."

"Thank you," Halligan said as he held the front door for Jean.

"It has been my pleasure, detectives," she said, nodding.

Then she started down the sidewalk and turned toward her home as Halligan closed the door.

Fawn just looked up at Halligan and those wonderful eyes of his, then said simply, "After that I'm going to need lunch. A big damn lunch."

"You and me both," Halligan said.

Fawn took the big black marker and marked "solved" on the file in her hand and put it in the main box.

Then without a word the two of them turned and headed out the door.

They had to call Andor and try to explain what they had just learned. But Fawn figured they could do that while eating.

CHAPTER THIRTY-FOUR

February 24th, 2019
Henderson, Nevada

Halligan got them to a small café tucked back in a strip mall on the other side of Highway 215 in Henderson. He loved the place mostly because their fries were to die for, and their burgers and sandwiches were supersized compared to most other places. Fawn had said she was hungry and he had decided he was as well.

The place consisted of ten booths along the left wall and a long counter along the right wall with a good twenty bar stools. Halligan's favorite booth in the back was open and he waved to a woman named Hanna who owned the place and she pointed to his booth with a smile.

Halligan really liked Hanna. She had bright red hair pulled back off her face and a smile with freckles that lit up the place. She was taller than he was by a ways and thin as a rail, which either meant she exercised a lot or didn't eat her own food. From the way she walked, he was betting on exercise.

"A regular here, huh?" Fawn asked as she slid into the booth with her back to the main door.

"I usually spread out paperwork in the booth," Halligan said. "Eat a huge lunch, and then sit for a few hours working as long as they are not full."

"This place is perfect for that," Fawn said.

Halligan glanced up at her smiling face, then shook his head. "Which booth do you use?"

"Front one," Fawn said. "But it's been a few months."

He just shook his head. The two of them were so similar in so many ways, it was scary.

"So they have you two working together, huh?" Hanna said as she put menus covered in plastic on their table, bringing with her the intense smell of fries.

"Both retired," Fawn said. "But still working and yes, together now."

"Great to hear," Hanna said, smiling.

They both ordered coffee and French dips, mostly because Fawn ordered it first and it sounded great and he hadn't had one for a while.

Then while their food was being prepped, they called Andor and told him everything, including the deal they had made with her to tell them if anyone started working one of her people's cases.

"Amazing first case for you two," Andor said. "Not only solved the one I gave you, but thirty-plus more and somehow managed to not find any dead people or mass graves along the way. Well done. Now I'm going to expect that every case."

"Uhh, no," Halligan said while Fawn laughed. "From now on out, it's dead bodies buried in the desert."

"Yeah," Fawn said. "We can't handle all this happy ending crap."

"I'm not dealing real well with it either," Andor said and then hung up.

They spent the next hour having a wonderful lunch, talking about different cases and old relationships.

Then, when they were all done, Halligan looked at Fawn and said, "Now what?"

"We go mark all those files closed," Fawn said. "And then we sit and see if we can figure out anything at all we are missing about all this before we shut it all down."

"Still not believing everything, huh?" Halligan asked.

Fawn shrugged. "I am, but too many years of being a detective and learning not to trust when something looks good that it might actually be good."

"Sounds like a plan to me," Halligan said. "I got a hunch there were a couple questions we missed."

"I have no doubt," Fawn said. "And I should have time to ask them in the morning.

CHAPTER THIRTY-FIVE

February 25th, 2019
Las Vegas, Nevada

The next morning Fawn found herself a few minutes before eight in the morning standing in front of the Starbucks in the massive hallway that led toward the Mandalay Convention Center from the main hotel and casino area.

Since the last time she had been in here, it had clearly been remodeled and expanded. The hallway ceilings were two stories overhead and even in a narrow spot it would take twenty paces to get across. And along the right side there were now numbers of restaurants and bars, all closed at this time of the morning, so the smell of Starbucks coffee just sort of smothered the wide hallway.

Thankfully, Fawn had brought her own coffee because the line of women lined up at Starbucks stretched a ways down the hall.

And a lot of other women were walking at a good pace

toward the convention center, all but a few wearing comfortable walking shoes. Fawn had realized this morning that running shoes might just be the right idea, since in this town convention centers almost always required a vast amount of walking.

So she had put on blue dress slacks, a white silk blouse with a blue jacket, and tennis shoes. She had her badge on the inside of her pocket, but had left her gun in her condo.

Jean Hult came up behind her and tapped her on the shoulder.

"Morning detective," she said. "Let's join the stream of women."

Fawn was glad to see that Jean had also brought a mug of coffee and was dressed very similar to Fawn, with slacks, a jacket, and comfortable walking shoes.

There had to be hundreds of women walking with them, and now Fawn understood why Jean had said that Halligan wouldn't fit in. There wasn't a man in the crowd.

And some of the women were walking hand-in-hand.

When they finally got to the massive convention center, Jean offered Fawn a program of the events.

"These are all seminars and smaller classes sponsored by ASR," Jean said. "I just want to show you a few that will be starting and then let you go your own way. But you are free to stay and attend if you would like."

"Thank you," Fawn said.

At that moment two women walked up to say good morning to Jean. After a moment Jean turned to Fawn. "Detective Fawn," Jean said. "I would like for you to meet Stephanie and Brenda. They are both from Salt Lake, but both worked for ASR at one time."

Fawn shook their hands, saying it was nice to meet them, managing to keep the feeling of shock off her face.

As they walked away, Jean said softly, "If you didn't recognize her, Stephanie was one of those files on Detective Halligan's table."

"Oh, I recognized her," Fawn said. "Had a hell of a time keeping on my poker face."

With that Jean led her through a large doorway into a room that had to hold a thousand chairs with a stage up front. The place was filling up quickly as Jean led the way along the side and up to the stage.

Fawn instantly recognized who they were headed toward. It was Sandy Goodson, their original missing person's case, the case that she had tried to solve on her own years before.

As they got closer, Sandy glanced up and smiled at Jean and Fawn.

"Sandy," Jean said. "I would like you to meet Detective Fawn."

"Retired," Fawn said as she smiled and shook Sandy's hand, something that seemed just completely surreal.

"Pleasure to meet you, detective," Sandy said. "I am very sorry my case caused you so much worry over the years. But I am honored you kept looking for me."

Now Fawn felt totally out of her element.

"This is my pleasure meeting you," Fawn said after glancing at the smiling face of Jean, then back at Sandy. "And seeing you are so happy and healthy. You can't believe what a relief that is for an experienced detective like me."

Sandy just beamed, then stepped forward and gave Fawn a hug. "Thank you so much for caring and keeping our secrets."

"Oh, trust me," Fawn said. "The pleasure is completely mine."

Sandy squeezed Fawn's hand, then said, "I'm about to start. Do take care and thank Detective Halligan for me as well."

"I will," Fawn said.

With that she and Jean headed back along the side of the almost full massive room to the back and out into the huge outer hall.

"Do they all know we were looking?" Fawn asked once they were away from everyone.

"No," Jean said. "Sandy is a VP for ASR and in charge of our large teaching programs. I kept her in the loop completely on what was happening with your investigation of her and the others. One of the others on your list worked in our computer department and she was also aware."

Fawn just looked around, trying to get her footing again. Women of all shapes and sizes and ages were headed toward different conference rooms.

"So all of this is teaching?" Fawn asked.

"And counseling. Sandy is teaching two large sessions today on how to deal with toxic family members."

"I assume by not vanishing," Fawn said.

"Not unless abusive or violently dangerous," Jean said. "We have trained women throughout the ballroom in there to watch for signs of abuse and find ways to talk privately with women who might need more help than they can get from notes in a class.

"This is all very impressive," Fawn said.

"Even with the new laws," Jean said, "the hate and anger and violence toward the LGBTQ community is actually growing and more out in the open. And that is especially true against women. So we do what we can."

Fawn just nodded. "Seems you do a great deal. And I most certainly want to thank you for opening my eyes as an old cop on my first case retired."

Jean just shook her head. "There you go with that old stuff. I thought that was just Halligan."

Fawn laughed and said, "Got me on that one. Fifty-five is not old."

"And I wouldn't let that partner of yours go without a fight," Jean said. "I can tell from his eyes and his questions and actions, he's one of the good ones."

"I'm quickly coming to agree with you on that."

Jean handed her a card. "My private number at the corporation. Call me at any time if you have a case that might fit in our area of expertise. We'll be glad to help where we can."

Fawn shook Jean's hand and thanked her. It looked like Fawn's and Halligan's team just grew by the resources of a major company if they needed it.

Fawn turned and headed back down the now almost empty large hallway toward the casino and the parking garage beyond.

Halfway down the hallway she reached Halligan on his phone.

"Breakfast?" she asked.

"Same place, same booth?"

"Absolutely."

"I'll have the coffee on the table waiting."

"Perfect," she said, and hung up.

Halligan was going to be as shocked as she felt with all this. And right now she needed breakfast with him.

And share all this amazing stuff.

After all, that's what partners of all types were for.

EPILOGUE

March 1st, 2019
Henderson, Nevada

Halligan stood in the empty condo's living room, the light from the beautiful day flooding in around him as he stared out over the Strip and the mountains beyond.

"Very similar to mine," Fawn said, coming out of the area of the two bedrooms and master bath suite.

It did look similar. Only Fawns had a much smaller kitchen and no formal dining area. And she had hers tastefully decorated in tan and browns and a wall of books in her living room.

She also had two large tables and a desk in her second bedroom that served as an office and more than likely he would do the same with this one.

Her condo wasn't more than a hundred paces down the hall and down one floor as well. They had talked a lot about living in the same building and they honestly both liked the idea.

This place smelled clean and he actually felt comfortable,

something he hadn't felt since Cindy died. He felt like maybe he had just found a home.

He turned from the living room window and went to the massive dining area in front of a window near the kitchen.

"Think the big table will fit here?"

"Absolutely," Fawn said. "Big table there pushed up against the wall under the window, smaller table in that nook with the view of the Strip."

He nodded to that. He could actually imagine it.

He had decided that after how well that big dining room table in his house had worked for their first case, he wanted to keep it. Not only for work, but for having more people over for dinner. For some reason, that idea appealed to him now. Never had in the last ten years, but now it did.

He turned to her and smiled. "One last time. Are you sure you want me this close?"

"Would make it a hell of a lot easier to bring the popcorn over for movie night."

He laughed and said, "Yes it would. So that's it, I'm buying it."

"Oh, fantastic," she said, coming up and giving him a huge hug, a beaming smile covering her face.

He liked the feel of that a lot. And her excitement about him living close.

"So you need to sell your house first?"

"Nope," he said. "Got more than enough in the bank."

"Wow, isn't that nice," she said.

"Do you even know how much you have in all your accounts?" he asked, smiling at her. "I bet more than enough to buy this with cash as well."

She laughed, looking embarrassed. "Yeah, maybe a couple times over."

He held out his arm. "Let's go talk with the sales agent and get this locked up. Then we got to get some dinner before we dare walk into that task force meeting tonight.

"Why is that?" she asked.

"Only a week and how quickly she forgets that thick smell of KFC."

"Oh, my, yes, dinner first."

"I know where there is a KFC just a mile from here," he said.

"No," she said, shaking her head. "I live in Vegas, a city full of great food."

He laughed. "I would have said the same thing if you suggested it."

"Great," she said. "Sushi."

"Reading my mind again," he said.

"It's a fun one to read."

And with that he pulled the door to his new condo closed behind them and they headed to get their second cold case as the newest members of the Cold Poker Gang task force.

More than likely, this one would have a dead body.

But with Fawn as his partner, nothing would surprise him.

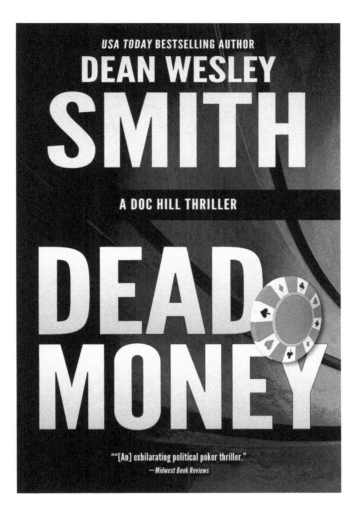

If you enjoyed Bottom Pair, *you might enjoy the book that inspired the entire Cold Poker Gang Mystery series,* Dead Money. *The following is a sample chapter from that book.*

THE GAME BEGINS

Poker is not a game of cards. It is a game of people.

PROLOGUE

Central Idaho Mountains. August 17, 2009

SILENCE.

Silence, the absolute worst thing a pilot can experience at seven thousand feet in a single-engine Piper 6XT. A moment before, the engine had filled the cockpit with a solid rumbling, a vibration-filled sound that Carson Hill knew from hundreds of hours of flight time.

The engine-monitoring system panel hadn't given him a warning. The plane had shaken with what had felt like a small explosion. Then everything on the control board had just snapped down to zero. Black smoke had poured out of the engine compartment, covering the front windows with a thin, black film.

Now the smoke was gone and through the film he could see the tree-covered ridgeline directly ahead.

The slight creaking of metal, the faint sound of the wind rushing past the six-seater's windows. Nothing else broke the deadly quiet.

He forced down the panic threatening to overwhelm him.

"Goddammit! What the hell happened?" His voice seemed extra loud.

He took a deep breath. Losing control now would just make sure he died.

In his hands, the plane's controls felt heavy, unresponsive. His dead-stick training was from a book and a few sentences from his original flight instructor over three decades ago. He had never actually flown a plane without a working engine.

Around him, the dark blue September sky contrasted with the green forests and brown rocks of the Idaho wilderness below. Normally, he loved this easy flight. He'd done it every year at the same time for longer than he wanted to admit. Now everything below him looked like a nightmare in the making, ready to reach out and tear him apart.

The ridgeline loomed ahead, a wall of death. He wasn't clearing that ridge.

He forced himself to take a deep breath. Then, with shaking hands, he fought to get the plane into a very slow turn.

Nothing wanted to move.

The trees ahead filled everything in his sight.

He kept fighting the controls, forcing the plane to turn by almost sheer will. It took every bit of his strength, as if the plane had a mind of its own and actually wanted to crash into the trees and rocks.

Everything seemed to slow down.

Finally, the trees were no longer growing threats filling his vision, but instead were flashing past the wing's tip.

He bet he didn't miss the tops of the pines by more than a few feet.

Somehow, between deep, sobbing breaths of oil-tainted air, he got the plane leveled and back over the deep valley, headed downstream. Sweat ran down his face and into his eyes as he tried the restart sequence.

Nothing.

With almost no control, no engine, no place to land but into trees and rocks, he was as good as dead.

He pushed that thought away and grabbed the radio mike. "Mayday! Mayday!"

Silence.

No response from either the McCall or Cascade, Idaho airports.

He clicked on the global positioning emergency beacon. At least Search and Rescue would find him quickly.

Ahead, the narrow valley floor closed down tighter and tighter. He couldn't be more than a thousand feet above the stream and dropping faster than he wanted to think about. It was taking every bit of his strength to keep the plane flying and not stalling.

He wiped the sweat off his face with his sleeve and tried to get a good look at what lay ahead through the oil-smeared window. Sharp rocks and thick forests covered everything. At this speed, and without any real control, the plane would be torn apart on impact.

"Need an opening," he said. "Just give me an opening." His

voice sounded loud and strained in the silence of the cockpit.

The valley narrowed ahead into a rock canyon, but over the edges of the rocks he could see a meadow beyond. If he could make the meadow, he might have a chance.

He tried to focus on the open area where the sun was shining, pushing the plane past the dark shadows of the rock canyon and into the light.

But he was dropping far too fast.

He tried feathering the controls to keep the plane up, but nothing seemed to work. Instead of something responsive in his hand, it felt like he was pushing against a stuck handle and pedals.

The rock walls now loomed ahead, a tiny opening leading to the sunshine beyond.

It was going to take a lot of luck to fit the plane through that narrow canyon opening. And after thirty-three years of playing professional poker, he didn't much believe in luck.

Then, quicker than he realized possible, he was in the canyon, the rocks flashing past. Ahead, the meadow seemed to call to him, the bright sunshine a beacon.

A tip of one wing caught the rock cliff face.

Before Carson had time to react or even cover his head and face, the small plane slammed into the rock wall.

Steven leaned against a tall pine in the shade, trying to stay cool, watching impassively as Carson Hill's plane struggled to stay in the air.

From Steven's position on the top of the major ridgeline

dividing the Cascade Valley from the central Idaho primitive area, he could see clear to the Middle Fork of the Salmon over thirty miles away. He had picked the spot just for that reason.

The day had turned beautiful, almost hot. He had waited patiently for six hours, slowly drinking bottles of water, until the signal had come in from the device he had planted in Carson's plane that told him Carson had started up his engine at the Scott airstrip deep inside the primitive area.

Steven felt no emotion as Carson Hill's six-seater Piper Cub barely escaped crashing into the hill below him. He simply watched as the plane drifted silently down the valley. Carson was full of all kinds of surprises. He shouldn't have been able to make that turn, not with his engine gone and his controls damaged in the small explosion Steven had set off in the plane's engine compartment.

The hillside below Steven had been the intended crash sight. More than likely the crash would still kill Carson, but it wasn't going to be close enough for Steven to retrieve Carson's key.

Steven shrugged. That was only a slight glitch in his plans. Too bad. He had wanted to take the key from Carson's dead, mangled body. There would have been a nice justice to that. But there would be other keys to give him that pleasure. There had been ten players in that poker game. Nine keys.

Steven dropped the small remote detonation device he had used to set off the explosion in Carson's plane into a three-foot-deep hole he had dug while waiting, then quickly filled the hole back up, covering it with pine needles. No point in carrying the device back down the mountain with him. No one would find it here, and even if they did, it couldn't be traced to him. He had left no detail to chance.

He trusted no one.

He had learned that lesson well.

Carson's key would survive the crash, and even with Carson dead, someone would have the key very shortly, then take Carson's position in the game.

If Steven had to kill that person, as well, so be it.

NEWSLETTER SIGN-UP

Be the first to know!

Just sign up for the Dean Wesley Smith newsletter, and keep up with the latest news, releases and so much more—even the occasional giveaway.

So, what are you waiting for? To sign up go to deanwesleysmith.com.

But wait! There's more. Sign up for the WMG Publishing newsletter, too, and get the latest news and releases from all of the WMG authors and lines, including Kristine Kathryn Rusch, Kristine Grayson, Kris Nelscott, *Smith's Monthly, Pulphouse Fiction Magazine,* and so much more.

To sign up go to wmgpublishing.com.

ABOUT THE AUTHOR

Considered one of the most prolific writers working in modern fiction, *USA Today* bestselling writer Dean Wesley Smith published almost two hundred novels in forty years, and hundreds and hundreds of short stories across many genres.

At the moment he produces novels in several major series, including the time travel Thunder Mountain novels set in the Old West, the galaxy-spanning Seeders Universe series, the urban fantasy Ghost of a Chance series, a superhero series starring Poker Boy, and a mystery series featuring the retired detectives of the Cold Poker Gang.

His monthly magazine, *Smith's Monthly*, which consists of only his own fiction, premiered in October 2013 and offers readers more than 70,000 words per issue, including a new and original novel every month.

During his career, Dean also wrote a couple dozen *Star Trek* novels, the only two original *Men in Black* novels, Spider-Man and X-Men novels, plus novels set in gaming and television worlds. Writing with his wife Kristine Kathryn Rusch under the name Kathryn Wesley, he wrote the novel for the NBC miniseries The Tenth Kingdom and other books for *Hallmark Hall of Fame* movies.

He wrote novels under dozens of pen names in the worlds of comic books and movies, including novelizations of almost a dozen films, from *The Final Fantasy* to *Steel* to *Rundown*.

Dean also worked as a fiction editor off and on, starting at Pulphouse Publishing, then at *VB Tech Journal*, then Pocket Books, and now at WMG Publishing, where he and Kristine Kathryn Rusch serve as series editors for the acclaimed *Fiction River* anthology series, which launched in 2013. In 2018, WMG Publishing Inc. launched the first issue of the reincarnated *Pulphouse Fiction Magazine*, with Dean reprising his role as editor.

For more information about Dean's books and ongoing projects, please visit his website at www.deanwesleysmith.com and sign up for his newsletter.